New York
New Year
New You

RACHAEL BLOOME
USA TODAY BESTSELLING AUTHOR

For Film & TV Rights: hello@rachaelbloome.com

Cover design: Mariah Sinclair

Editing: Krista Dapkey with KD Proofreading

Proofing: Beth Attwood

For Melissa,
The original creator of MAD Market & the best sister ever.

LETTER FROM THE AUTHOR

~

Dear Reader,

Sometimes, a story appears in our mind so vivid and fully formed, it begs to be told. That's what happened with this story. I heard Quincy's voice in my head, and no matter how often or adamantly I tried to quiet her, she simply wouldn't stop talking. So, despite a jam-packed writing schedule and two other novels ahead of Quincy's in the production line, I agreed to tell her story first. I guess it pays to be a chatterbox.

While this may not have been the story you expected me to write next, I hope this stand-alone speaks to your heart in the same way my series does, with all the warmth and fondness of sitting down for coffee with a good friend.

Blessings & Blooms,

Rachael Bloome

1

If someone ever filmed my family at Christmastime, the end result would resemble a reality show where siblings are pitted against each other in a series of to-the-death competitions. Either that, or a documentary on domestic dysfunction with a delightfully festive backdrop. I can even hear the voice-over narration announcing "The Carmichael clan competes for the Christmas crown" with exaggerated alliteration.

Observing what I've now dubbed the Gingerbread Gauntlet, I pop a gumdrop in my mouth, letting the copious amounts of sugar dissolve on my tongue as I regard my brother's pièce de résistance. Matt has captured Thomas Jefferson's historic home, the Monti-cello, in impressive detail down to the candy cane columns.

Beside him, my sister, Veronica, painstakingly

squeezes a piping bag, adding evenly spaced frosting shingles to a fairy-tale cottage tantalizing enough to tempt Hansel and Gretel, even after their ill-fated foray into the witch's forest.

By the end of the day, my dad will choose this year's winner who will receive—I kid you not—a literal trophy. It's one of those plastic statues passed out like candy at the end of a children's soccer tournament, but still... It's a trophy. For the best gingerbread house. Because who makes a gingerbread house just for fun?

If I sound bitter, it's not because in all my twenty-eight years of life, I've never won the trophy. Or even come close. No, the slight chip on my shoulder is because, just once, I'd like to celebrate the holidays like I'm in one of those Hallmark movies with my loving family gathered around a cozy fireplace singing carols while big, fluffy snowflakes flutter outside the frosted window.

But that will never happen. Because my family can't sing carols without turning it into a Christmas episode of *The Voice*. And it never snows in Los Angeles.

Veronica sets down the icing and reaches for the sifter of powdered sugar to add a dusting of saccharine snow to her creation. Her hand collides with Matt, who had the same idea.

"Excuse me, but I'm using that." Veronica tightens her grip on the sifter.

"Correction. *I'm* using it." Matt gives a little tug, eliciting a puffy white cloud.

I lean back in my chair, nibbling on a Twizzler as I watch the scene unfold. Even though they're both in their early thirties, Veronica and Matt bicker like toddlers. Unless they're picking on me, of course. That's a united effort.

"No, *I* am." Veronica gives the handle a hard yank, and a powdery plume explodes across the table like a sweetly scented volcanic eruption.

"Great. Look what you did." Matt brushes the front of his cable-knit sweater, but only manages to make a bigger mess.

Watching in amusement, I drag the unchewed end of my licorice stick through the silky coating covering the plaid tablecloth, absentmindedly tracing an outline of a snow angel.

"Me?" Veronica cries indignantly. "This is *your* fault! Look what you did to my gingerbread house. You buried it under an avalanche."

"Yeah, well, mine looks like it was obliterated by a blizzard. So, I guess we're even," Matt huffs.

Veronica pouts for a full thirty seconds before her lips curl into a smirk. "Well, I guess it could be worse. Our gingerbread houses could look like Quincy's. What's it supposed to be, anyway? A replica of the Roman ruins?"

Matt snorts. "Don't be obtuse. Can't you tell she's making an artistic statement?"

"Oh, right." Veronica nods, playing up the joke.

"What's your masterpiece called?" she asks me with mock sincerity. "*Deconstructed Gingerbread House*?"

They share a laugh.

"Ha-ha. You two are hilarious." I roll my eyes and take a nonchalant bite of the Twizzler, forgetting I'd just dipped it in sugar. *Gross.* There really is such a thing as too sweet.

I'd like to say their insults are out of jealousy, but the truth is, my gingerbread house—if you can even call it a house—would be condemned by any self-respecting building inspector. I doubt the lopsided roof could withstand a light throat-clearing from the Big Bad Wolf, let alone a full-blown huff and puff. But you want to know the truly sad part? It's probably my best attempt to date. I am not gifted in the fine art of transforming baked goods into a home befitting the Borrowers.

I push back my chair and stand.

"Come on, Quincy. We're only teasing. Don't leave," Veronica cajoles, doing her best to appear contrite. "We'll be good. Right, Matt?"

"Scout's honor." He raises three fingers in the Boy Scout salute, even though he was never a member.

For a moment, I consider sitting back down. Despite the lifetime that has proven otherwise, a small part of me wants to believe in a Christmas miracle—that for once, we can enjoy a holiday together without the back-handed insults lobbed in my direction like verbal snow-balls. Snowballs with hidden rocks in the center.

But before I can decide my next move, Mom sashays

out of the kitchen carrying a silver platter of her infamous fruitcake. I know the iconic dessert gets a lot of flak this time of year, and the wisecracks are endless, but when it comes to my mother's recipe, they're all true. It's basically concrete in loaf form, sprinkled with a few dried cranberries that, frankly, deserve better.

"Okay, kids. Time for fruitcake," she announces in a singsong voice.

Matt and Veronica unabashedly groan, and my mother's smile falters.

Deidre Carmichael has only one flaw. And it's her inedible fruitcake. But despite the fact that one bite could crack the toughest of tooth enamel, she puts her heart and soul into it every year.

"Thanks, Mom." I lift a hefty slice off the serving plate, nearly spraining my wrist. It easily weighs five pounds. "I've been waiting for this all night."

Okay, so I've actually been *anxiously* awaiting it like a dental patient thumbing through a tattered copy of *Highlights* magazine before their root canal, but I don't expound on that detail.

Her face brightens. "Thank you, sweetheart."

I follow her into the living room where my dad reclines in his wingback chair in front of the fire, both feet propped on a matching brocade ottoman. An unlit cigar dangles from between his lips. He claims he enjoys the smell and mouthfeel, but I've long suspected it's simply an excuse to avoid eating Mom's fruitcake.

I settle in the middle of the emerald Edwardian-style velvet sofa, which I honestly don't think was ever intended to be used as furniture, and Matt and Veronica plop down on either side of me.

Mom sets the fruitcake on the coffee table and offers me another slice. Her expression is so innocently expectant, I can't refuse even though my stomach is still trying to figure out what to do with the first one.

Veronica snickers under her breath, but I ignore her, happy to see the glow on Mom's face as she serves everyone eggnog before joining Dad in the twin armchair by the hearth.

The comforting sound of crackling logs mingles with the soft, melodic notes of "White Christmas" emanating from the custom built-in speakers hidden in the mantelpiece. The entire scene, from the tasteful decorations to everyone's designer Christmas sweaters, is worthy of a greeting card. Yet, my chest constricts with a familiar foreboding, full of dread for what comes next.

"As we draw near the end of another year," Dad says, raising his crystal-etched punch glass, "I couldn't be prouder of all we've accomplished. The Carmichaels are a force to be reckoned with."

"Hear! Hear!" Matt chants, lifting his own glass in solidarity.

As my father's appraising gaze sweeps over us, I shrink back into the rock-hard cushions, wishing I could sink into the crevices and disappear. My dad, Charles Carmichael III, tends to have that effect on people. He expects nothing less than excellence. Of everyone. Which is probably why his advertising firm, Carmichael Creatives, has achieved such an impressive level of success. But no one feels the spine-crushing pressure more than his offspring.

"Deidre," he says, turning to my mother, "the chest, please."

She ceremoniously hands him an antique writing box of brass-bound mahogany, the sort of box I imagine British soldiers used to send love letters to their betrothed back home. Five scrolls lie inside, along with five gold-plated Montblanc pens.

Matt and Veronica scoot toward the edge of the couch in eager anticipation, while I retreat farther back, craning my neck in search of an escape. Am I too young to fake a convincing stroke? I glance at the fruitcake. What if I nibble another bite and it conveniently lodges in my throat? Would choking to death extricate me from this unbearable situation? Or will I still be expected to participate as the paramedics wheel away my lifeless body on a gurney?

Probably the latter.

While I resign myself to the inevitable, Mom passes out the scrolls.

"Matthew," Dad says, "as the eldest, you go first."

Matt sits up straighter, pulling his shoulders so far back I can't help but wonder if they popped out of socket. If so, he doesn't seem to notice. "Last year," he says with a self-gratified grin, "my Christmas Commitment was to learn Japanese. *Ninmu kanryō*." He presses his palms together and bows at the waist as Mom and Veronica applaud and Dad voices his approval.

Since before I was born, my family has carried out a tradition called Christmas Commitments. Because we can't simply make New Year's resolutions like normal people. It's essentially the same thing except a week earlier. And we write them down and report back each year, which is apparently all part of the "fun."

"Veronica?" Dad prompts, beaming at her proudly.

She tosses her hair over her shoulder, whipping me in the face. Fortunately, she had her hair professionally blow-dried for the occasion, so the icy-blond strands are silky soft and emit her trademark scent—strawberries and superiority.

"My Christmas Commitment was to get my master's degree in business communications." She pauses for dramatic effect, then draws a large swish in the air with her finger and says, "Check!"

"Well done!" This time, Dad starts the round of applause.

After she's been duly praised, the room turns eerily silent save for the melancholy rendition of "A Change at Christmas" by the Flaming Lips and the aforementioned crackling logs. I can feel the pitying glances, although I keep my eyes glued to the festive Nordic print on my fuzzy socks. The alternating pattern of tree, snowflake, tree, snowflake is quite hypnotic if you stare at it hard enough.

"Quincy?" I can hear the hesitation in my father's voice. And something even sadder—hope. After all these years, he still thinks there's a chance I won't completely disappoint him.

My throat tightens. "I, uh..."

"It's okay, honey," Mom coos in her coddling way. The way that says *All my babies are perfect, no matter what. Even you, Quincy.* "You can tell us."

"Come on." Veronica nudges my arm. "How bad can it be?"

What she means to say is *It can't be any worse than every year prior.* And she's right. I take a deep breath, but I can't form the words.

"Oh, for goodness' sake," she groans in exasperation. "I'll do it." Leaning over my shoulder, she reads off my scroll. "Last year, you wrote *take a dance class.*" She looks up, baffled. "That's it? That's your easiest Christmas Commitment ever. What were you so worried about? You didn't even specify that you had to be any *good* at it."

"Yeah, Quincy," Matt adds, placing a hand on my arm. "I'm sure you were able to take a simple dance class, right?"

Heat and humiliation creep up my neck. I *almost* did. But when I arrived at Introduction to Swing in a 1950s rockabilly outfit only to find everyone else in street clothes, I was so embarrassed, I quickly ducked out of the room. Then I kind of... forgot about it.

When I don't respond, my mother and father

exchange a look. A look that simultaneously fills me with shame and relief as Mom chirps, "Why don't I go next?"

For several minutes following, I barely listen as my parents take turns reporting on their accomplishments. Ever since I was five and quit ballet after one lesson, it's become a family joke that I never follow through on anything. The adorable nickname Quincy the Quitter has been bandied about more than a few times. I'm not sure if it's a chicken-and-egg situation and I quit things to live up to the moniker, or if I earned the title because I always quit things, but either way... The charming epithet will probably be engraved on my headstone.

"Anyway, kids," Dad says, "that's my big announcement."

I blink, realizing I've missed something important. "What announcement?"

"Jeez, Quincy. Aren't you paying attention?" Veronica sighs loudly. "Steve Bailcroft is retiring, and Dad wants to promote either Matt or me to marketing director. We have three months to create a campaign for our new client, Extra Energy Drink. Whoever comes up with the winning pitch gets the promotion."

For a moment, I'm too stunned to speak. Steve Bailcroft has been Dad's right-hand man at Carmichael Creatives since its inception. He's credited with more successful ad campaigns than anyone else in the company. Of course, Matt and Veronica have coveted his position since the day they were hired straight out of college, but everyone—including myself—thought Steve would keel over mid–pitch meeting before he ever retired. I guess we underestimated the powerful—and undeniably adorable—draw of his grandkids in Idaho.

Without thinking, I blurt, "What about me?"

Veronica bursts into laughter, and I can't blame her. I have no idea what came over me. Except, I have this sudden, all-consuming urge to change the course of my life. Like Scrooge being shown his dismal fate by the Ghost of Christmas Yet to Come, I glimpsed my own depressing future and didn't like what I saw.

Veronica quickly sobers when I don't recant my question. "Wait, are you serious?"

"Why not? I've worked there nearly as long as you have. And I'm a pretty decent copywriter."

"Sure, but..." She trails off as if her objections should be obvious, and casts a "can you believe her?" expression in Dad's direction.

He steeples his fingers and presses them to his chin, mulling it over.

"Daddy, please don't tell me you're actually considering Quincy for the position. Even if she wins, she'll quit a day later," Veronica voices what everyone's thinking.

After a beat, Dad lowers his fingers and meets my gaze. "Veronica makes a valid point. How can I be assured you'll follow through if you win?"

I hesitate, admittedly stumped. I'd give him my

word, but it doesn't mean all that much when you consider my track record.

"I know!" Veronica cries, snatching the scroll from my hand. "What if she has to finish her Christmas Commitments? *All* of them?" Her eyes flash with a devious triumph, and for a moment, I marvel at how two people can look so much alike—we share the same lapis-blue eyes and blond hair, though mine is more sunny than snow queen—but be polar opposites in every other way.

As Dad ruminates over her suggestion, my pulse sputters. Maybe I could complete one or two of the items on the list, but *all* of them in three months? There's no way.

"That's not a bad idea, Veronica," Dad says, and my heart plummets. "But not the entire list." He turns to me. "If you want to be taken seriously in this competition, over the next three months, you'll need to finish the last ten items on your list, including whatever you add today. Do we have a deal?"

I glance between Matt and Veronica. Matt licks his thumb and rubs the remaining powdered sugar smudge on his sweater, wholly uninterested, like he knows I'll fail and isn't worried about it. But Veronica... Veronica has this slightly manic glint in her eye, and her lips curl into a challenging sneer.

"I'll do it," I say quickly before I can stop myself.

"Excellent!" Dad raises his glass. "Then may the best Carmichael win."

As everyone salutes with a sip of eggnog, Veronica traces her fingertip down my list, landing on the first item I'll need to cross off—the one I wrote ten years ago.

A slow smile spreads across her face as she leans in and whispers, "Good luck, Quincy. New York City is going to eat you alive."

2

I dig my nails into the disconcertingly sticky leather seat as the cab driver swerves around a pedestrian with a death wish, wondering if Veronica was right.

This New York, with the petulant gray sky and gritty slush covering the uneven sidewalk, isn't the magical city of Nora Ephron films. Although, it's probably my fault. If I'd arrived in autumn rather than early January, I'd be sniffing bouquets of sharpened pencils instead of shivering in my too-thin coat, regretting my life choices.

The cabby—who's inexplicably averse to modern comforts like a heater and air freshener—slams on the brakes, and my forehead flies forward, colliding with the front seat headrest, which is slimy for unfathomable reasons. *Ick.*

He hammers his fist against the horn, glaring at a stylish woman weighed down with shopping bags who'd stepped off the Fifth Avenue curb without a moment's thought to oncoming traffic. Somehow, she manages to maneuver her belongings just enough to free her hand for an offensive gesture that elicits a round of obscenities in return.

Ah, New York. The city that never sleeps. Which explains why everyone is so crabby.

I'm thrown back against the seat as the driver stomps on the gas, grumbling something about lousy tourists under his breath. I consider apologizing on behalf of myself and my fellow sojourners, but decide to keep my mouth shut, figuring anonymity is my best shot at survival. But I seriously contemplate booking a return flight as soon as I arrive at Brynn's place. My childhood best friend would be disappointed but would ultimately understand. That's the one perk to being dubbed Quincy the Quitter... no one bats an eye when you bail.

After all, I'd done that very thing ten years ago when I'd promised to follow her to New York after my gap year. She'd gone off to college at Columbia, and except for the one summer I'd visited—aka the worst summer of my life—I abandoned the idea of joining her. Eventually, she stopped asking me.

When I'd called out of the blue after the new year and sheepishly told her about the competition and asked to stay with her for three months—since Dad decreed it would be long enough to cross "Move to New York" off my list—I'd half expected her to hang up before I'd finished my sentence. I hadn't exactly done a great job keeping in touch all those years. But I should have known better. Brynn has always been the sweetest, most forgiving person on the planet, and she genuinely seems excited to see me. Which, I'm not gonna lie, adds to my guilt.

The cab lurches to a stop outside a stately brick building that looks more like a swanky hotel than an apartment complex. *This* is where Brynn lives?

Light snowflakes begin to fall, swirling around the black-and-white-striped awning shielding the entrance and dusting the twin rows of potted conifer trees flanking the broad stone steps. A soft glow emanates from behind the glass door like a beacon of warmth welcoming me out of the cold.

My spirits are so lifted by the beautiful sight, I don't even mind when the driver makes me haul my own humongous suitcase out of the trunk. Or when one of the wheels gets caught in a crack in the sidewalk. As freezing flakes find their way down my collar, stinging the back of my neck, I yank the handle of my suitcase, but it won't budge. I glance at the driver, hoping he'll take pity on my plight.

Instead, he skids off down the street, flinging ice-cold slush from his tires like a water cannon, drenching the front of my coat and jeans. To add insult to injury, my suitcase wheel chooses that exact moment to free itself from the crevice, and the momentum sends me flailing backward into a snow-covered—and unpleasantly prickly—bush.

For a moment, I consider the pros and cons of staying put and letting the thorny branches envelop me until I freeze solid and become a permanent fixture. Con: I'd probably be a prime spot for snooty Upper East Side dogs to relieve themselves. Pro: Becoming an ice sculpture may be my best shot at sticking out the entire three months in Manhattan. That settles it. Succumb to a frosty grave and finally finish what I started.

My resolve wavers when melted snow seeps through my clothing, shaking my body with a bone-shattering shiver. I clearly don't have what it takes to be a martyr for my own moral growth, so I ungracefully liberate myself.

Sopping wet and bedraggled, I lug my suitcase into the pristine lobby, dripping water onto the white marble floor. Taking in the elegant wallpaper and expensive artwork, I feel incredibly out of place as I try to remember Brynn's most recent text.

So sorry! I'm stuck at work. See
Sharon. And don't forget depreciation.

Her cryptic instructions don't make much sense, and I'm pretty sure that last part—which sounds like one of her nerdy accounting terms—is a mistake and meant for someone else.

Panic starts to set in. I should call her and ask for clarification, but I hate to bother her at work, especially since she's doing me such a gigantic favor. Maybe I can camp out in the lobby until she gets home?

Tiny tears of exhaustion and frustration build behind my eyes. I'm cold, travel-weary, and starving. The trifecta of emotional meltdowns.

"Can I help you?"

Through blurry vision, I spot a middle-aged woman in a black bellhop suit and shiny uniform hat covering her short-cropped brown hair. She looks like some sort of fancy concierge, further cementing my suspicion that Brynn actually lives in a posh boutique hotel.

"I'm looking for Brynn Delaney's apartment?"

"Ah, you must be Miss Carmichael." The woman smiles, deepening the wrinkles around her kind eyes and wide, friendly mouth. "I'm Sharon. Miss Delaney asked me to give this to you." She reaches into her breast pocket and withdraws a small white envelope. "This key is to 5C on the fifth floor. You can take the elevator, then turn right, and it's three doors down. Can I help with your luggage?"

"Thank you, but I can manage it." I peer inside the envelope and see a sparkling gold key.

"Is there anything else I can do for you?" Sharon asks warmly.

"No, thank you." All I can think about is taking a long, hot shower and raiding Brynn's refrigerator.

"Enjoy your stay." Sharon taps the brim of her hat before returning to her post by the front door. In my discombobulation, I must have walked right past her without realizing it.

My damp soles squeak across the floor as I drag my bag to the gilded elevator, and I can only imagine what Sharon must think of Brynn's out-of-town houseguest. I try to put my embarrassment out of my mind the entire ride to the fifth floor, but my cheeks still feel pink when I stick the key in the lock.

However, any thought I've ever had evaporates the second the door swings open, swept away by pure, jaw-dropping disbelief.

Brynn's apartment gleams like a glittering oasis in a metropolitan wilderness. You know how people say they want to pinch themselves in case they're actually dreaming? Yeah, that's the last thing I want to do. If this is a dream, sign me up for a lifetime's supply of Ambien.

I flick on the light and step farther into the foyer, marveling at the vast, open spaces. I thought all New Yorkers lived in shoeboxes. Sure, some might be Christian Louboutin or Manolo Blahnik, but shoeboxes, nonetheless.

Brynn's entryway opens to a sizable kitchen on the right and steps down to an even more expansive living room with a fireplace, huge flatscreen TV, and miles of built-in bookcases, which I plan to peruse to my heart's content later.

But my favorite feature? The three floor-to-ceiling picture windows framing a breathtaking view of the city all bathed in a bluish haze like a wintry wonderland. I can even glimpse the snowcapped trees of Central Park through the slits in the surrounding buildings.

I'm so mesmerized that, for a moment, I can't move. I can't even breathe. Instead, I concentrate on imprinting the scene into my permanent memory.

I knew Brynn did well for herself as a top-level CPA in a prestigious financial firm. She had such high-profile clients, they were protected by nondisclosure agreements. But I didn't know she did *this* well. Bravo, my friend. Bravo.

It's quite possible I would have stood in that spot, captivated by the view, for hours, completely forgetting my long-anticipated shower, if not for a low, guttural growl. The hairs on my arms shoot straight up, almost as quickly as my heart catapults into my throat.

Slowly, I turn toward the source of the sound.

A monstrous dog, almost mythical in size, engulfs the shadowy hallway. It reminds me a little of Beethoven from all those movies I watched as a kid. What kind of dog was he again? A Saint Bernard? I think that's it. Except, this dog has fangs that could fillet me in seconds.

"H-hey there, girl." I hold up my hands like a bank robber surrounded by a heavily armed SWAT team.

I'm met with another menacing growl.

When Veronica said New York City would eat me alive, I hadn't thought she'd meant literally.

"B-boy?" I stammer, worried I'd accidentally offended him. Was a dog more likely to maul you if you got its gender wrong? I'm not sure, but I don't really want to find out, either.

"Who's a good boy?" I ask feebly. My high-pitched, trepidatious tone resembles a preschool teacher who's afraid of children. The dog isn't impressed and curls his upper lip in a vicious snarl.

I have no idea what to do.

The ironic thing is I've always wanted a dog. For my fifth birthday, I'd begged my parents for a puppy, but thanks to Matt's allergies, they gave me a goldfish instead. I named him Spot, which suited him perfectly since he had a big white circle on the left side of his body. I'd strap his fishbowl into the seat of my little umbrella stroller and take him for walks. I even taught him a few tricks.

The only two he learned with any level of competency were "stay" and "play dead." And every time he successfully executed the last trick, his namesake spot would inexplicably be in a different location the next day. I don't want to admit how old I was when I finally figured out the *real* trick, which involved a punch card at the local pet store and my parents' uncanny ability to lie straight-faced.

Of course, I could have adopted a dog when I moved out, but I live alone in a tiny apartment in Burbank, and it doesn't seem right to keep an animal cooped up most of the day.

I wonder if I explain all of this to Cujo if he'll have mercy on me. Then a thought hits me. Depreciation!

The last word from Brynn's text. Snippets from one of our phone calls weave in and out of my jet-lagged brain as I struggle to find focus. I'd been busy trying to book my flight, so I only caught half of what she'd said.

I'm not entirely certain my recollection is correct, but it's worth a try.

"D-depreciation?" I whisper, praying this works.

His bushy reddish-brown eyebrows lift slightly. That's a good sign.

"Depreciation," I say again, this time a little louder and with more confidence.

The dog lunges toward me, and in my terror, I scrunch my eyes shut and fall to my knees, covering my face with both hands.

So, this is how it ends....

Two enormous paws topple me backward, but instead of ripping out my jugular, my attacker lathers me with an inch of slobber.

I force my eyes open and gaze into the most adorable, droopy brown eyes I've ever seen. The ferocious beast has transformed into a two-hundred-pound lapdog. I can't help but laugh.

"Hey, buddy. Are we friends now?" I scratch behind his soft, oversized ears, then notice the collar around his neck.

"Wilson," I add, reading the engraving.

He wiggles his backside in greeting.

"Hey, Wilson. I'm Quincy. Thanks for not eating me."

He nuzzles my face, and is so sweet and cuddly, I can't believe I was ever afraid of him.

"As much as I appreciate the sponge bath," I say as he licks my face again, "I'm in desperate need of a hot shower."

My phone buzzes in my coat pocket, and I dig it out to read the text from Brynn.

> Still working. So sorry you're spending your first night alone. Help yourself to the food in the fridge, including the leftover sushi. And don't wait up. It's going to be another all-nighter.

I text back.

> No worries. Wilson and I are best buds. See you in the morning.

As much as I'm looking forward to seeing Brynn, I don't mind turning in early. That is, after I wash up and avail myself of her leftovers.

I give Wilson a few more head scratches to solidify our new bond, then wander down the hall, vaguely recalling Brynn's description of where I'd find the guest bedroom.

It's technically her office, as denoted by the sleek, modern-style desk beneath the large window, but there's also a cozy daybed and a sumptuous-looking armchair tucked into a reading nook of sorts. The decor consists mostly of monochromatic neutrals with a few pops of rose-petal pink, and I couldn't have asked for a more pleasant space, even if I'd designed it myself.

After I dig a pair of pajamas out of my suitcase, I meander back down the hall in search of the guest bathroom.

Like everything else in Brynn's apartment, it's surprisingly spacious. And rather than a tub-and-shower combo with questionably colored grout—like the one in my bathroom—this is one of those walk-in designs with solid slate tile walls.

There's a stack of folded towels on a sleek metal rack, and I grab the one on top. It's as thick and plush as any you'd find at a five-star spa, and I unabashedly rub my cheek against the fluffy fabric, inhaling the distinct lavender scent.

My first night in New York might have gotten off to a rocky start, but it's slowly looking brighter.

Towel in hand, I step through the narrow opening and peel off my damp boots and clothes, placing them —and the cloudlike towel—on the teak bench at the back of the shower so they don't create a pool of water on the bathroom floor. The recessed lights in the ceiling cast a soft, soothing glow, and I can already feel some of the tension draining from my stiff muscles.

That is, until I spot the dozen or more showerheads protruding from all angles, including directly overhead. *Yeesh*. I might need an engineering degree just to figure out how to turn them all on.

As I'm analyzing which lever goes to which shower-head, the bathroom door creaks open.

My pulse spikes, then skitters to a halt.

I'm positive I closed the door behind me. I even remember hearing the latch click into place. Unless Wilson knows how to turn a door handle...

Fear creeps up my neck, and I shiver.

Brynn is still at work, so who could it be?

3

I snatch the towel off the bench and wrap it around myself. When CSI finds my body, at least I won't be in my birthday suit.

Biting my lip, I suppress a whimper as the prowler's heavy soles plod across the bathroom floor.

Is it possible I narrowly escaped Wilson's bone-crunching mandibles only to wind up like Janet Leigh's iconic character in Hitchcock's *Psycho*?

I've heard about New York's horrific crime rates, but I didn't think I'd become one of the statistics... especially on my first night!

Good grief. I'm so terrified, my thoughts are rambling.

Focus, Quincy. There's still a chance it's merely a burglar and he—or she—doesn't even know you're here.

Although, it begs the question... how did they get

past Wilson? I say a silent prayer he's unharmed. Maybe they tossed him a large steak to distract him?

The toilet seat clinks against the porcelain tank, and I jump in fright.

Is the... is the burglar using the bathroom?

I suppose even criminals have to go sometime. But here? Now?

This can't be happening.

For some reason, I close my eyes and cover my ears. Maybe it's from years of deeply ingrained propriety. Or perhaps I simply don't want the last sounds I hear before my demise to be a stranger's bodily functions. Either way, I inch backward, putting as much distance as possible between myself and the intruder. But as I quietly shuffle my feet, I bump one of the knobs and ice-cold water rains down on my head.

Before I can stop myself, I let out a yelp.

"Is someone in here?" a startled voice asks.

A startled voice I faintly recognize. But it can't be him... *can* it? "E-Ethan?" I squeak as I fumble with the slippery faucet with one hand while the other clutches the now-drenched towel.

"Quincy?"

I hear the distinct zip of his fly closing, which only adds to my embarrassment. What in the world is Brynn's older brother doing here?

"I didn't think you were arriving until tomorrow." His tone is sheepish and apologetic.

"Um, well..." I finally manage to shut the water off,

although droplets continue to bead off the ends of my hair and ping onto the tile floor. "I'm here now," I finish feebly, stating the obvious.

"Of course." He releases a self-chastising groan. "I'm sorry, Q. You're trying to take a shower, and I barged in here like a clueless idiot. I must have startled you to death. I'll go use Brynn's bathroom."

I take a moment to collect myself. He hasn't called me Q since... Well, since I visited Brynn in New York ten years ago. Why does the sound still send tingles down my spine?

I inhale sharply. Stop being ridiculous. Now is not the time to revisit a silly childhood crush.

"Thanks," I murmur, trying to repress my mortification. I never thought the first time I ran into Ethan again I'd be wrapped in a soaking-wet towel like some sort of soggy burrito, talking to him through a tile wall.

Even after the latch clicks shut, I hold my breath, not daring to move until I'm a thousand percent sure he's gone. And even then, my shower is hardly relaxing. Every little sound—plus some nonexistent ones—gives me a mini panic attack, although I know I'm being unnecessarily paranoid.

After I dry off, I slip into my flannel pajamas, regretting my pattern choice. I *could* have gone with tasteful snowflakes or plaid, but instead, I chose cartoonish cups of hot chocolate with cheesy smiles and their equally nonsensical winking marshmallow companions.

For a moment, I consider ducking into the guest room to change into my fleece-lined leggings, which even Veronica begrudgingly admitted make my back-side look "decent." Maybe I'll swipe on some mascara and lip gloss, too.

Ultimately, I decide to face Ethan in my mortifying PJs sans makeup. After all, my crush on Brynn's brother was a long time ago. We're adults now. He's probably married. Or seeing someone, at the very least. And I've sworn off dating for the next millennia or more.

I shove my feet into a pair of pink slipper socks—complete with wooly pom-poms on the backs—and pad softly into the kitchen. As soon as I round the corner, I regret my decision.

Ethan stands at the gas range with his back to me, stirring something heavenly in a small copper saucepan. I have a suspicion it's his family's decadent hot chocolate recipe—the kind his mother used to make Brynn and me after we played outside all day in the cold —but for once, it's not the chocolate that's making my mouth water.

Ethan's wearing loose sweats hanging low on his hips and a long-sleeve thermal shirt snug enough to show off the curve of his biceps. Wowza. Even when he ran cross-country in high school and worked out every day he never looked like *that*. All of a sudden, my mouth goes dry like one of my socks was stuffed in it.

Thankfully, Wilson barrels across the room and knocks some sense into me—literally and figuratively.

From my new position on the floor, I wrap my arms around his neck and give him a snuggle.

"Sorry about that," Ethan says on Wilson's behalf. "He doesn't realize how big he is."

"I don't mind." I bury my face in his fur to avoid looking at Ethan. For some reason, my stomach won't stop somersaulting. Maybe your first crush is like riding a bike? You never forget how badly it hurt the first time you fell.

"I still feel like a jerk for barging in on your first night in New York, so I made you my mother's cure-all as a peace offering."

The intoxicating aroma of rich dark chocolate draws my attention to Ethan as he slowly pours the thick, velvety liquid into two mugs.

My heartbeat slows at the sight of him. His caramel-colored hair is a little longer than it used to be, with a slight curl at the ends. But his hazel eyes have the same mischievous sparkle, and the left side of his mouth still lifts slightly higher than the right when he smiles, to devastating effect.

Breathe, Quincy. Just breathe.

"Thanks." Self-conscious, I tuck a strand of damp hair behind my ear and follow him into the living room.

I notice the fireplace first. Although it appears to be electric, the flames are surprisingly realistic and provide a pleasant amber glow along with a remarkable amount of heat. Against the wintry backdrop of New York City covered in snow, the idyllic scene is cozy and inviting.

Then my gaze lands on the coffee table. It's covered in a smorgasbord of snacks. Plates piled high with a variety of crackers and dips, plus a fondue set with melted cheese and chunks of artisan bread. And the holy grail: Brynn's leftover sushi.

"I thought you might be hungry." He sets the mugs on the coffee table and grabs a bag of marshmallows, ripping open the seal. "They're not the winking variety, but I thought we could roast them over the fondue flames later." He casts an impish glance at my pajamas, and I blush.

"Very funny." I hide my embarrassment by stuffing my face with a cracker dipped in a tangy red pepper hummus. All hope of making a good impression is already out the window, so I might as well relax and be myself. "Thank you," I mumble with my mouth full. "I'm starving."

Ethan unfurls a throw blanket for us to share while I fill my plate with an assortment of sushi rolls and sit cross-legged on the couch. Wilson leaps onto the cushion beside me, resting his boulder-sized head on my lap.

My heart only skips a little bit when Ethan sits next to me, slipping beneath one corner of the blanket close enough to smell his cedar-scented bodywash. Counting the subdued palpitation as progress, I forgo the chopsticks and start polishing off the spicy crab rolls like finger food. They may be the best thing I've ever tasted.

"What time did you get in?" Ethan asks, helping himself to a slice of sashimi.

"Just in time to avoid the storm of the century." I glance out the window at the quickly falling snow. "Will Brynn get home okay?"

"She'll be fine. We're used to this kind of weather."

As he dips his salmon in soy sauce, my mind reels with a million questions. Does he still live in New York, or is he only visiting? I don't see a ring, so he's not married, but is he seeing anyone? And what is he doing in Brynn's apartment? He clearly has a key, so...

Before I can ask, he says, "I think it's really cool you're staying with us for a few months. Brynn hasn't stopped talking about it since you called. Although, she wasn't sure you'd actually show up."

That stings a bit, but I deserve it. The truth is, I almost didn't. Last night I couldn't sleep. My thoughts were filled with every possible way I could fail, and all the reasons I should just give up now. Then Brynn texted telling me how excited she was, and I couldn't do it. I couldn't let her down again, so I—

Hang on a second! *What* did he say? "Us?" I repeat when his words finally click.

"Yeah, me and Brynn." He shoots me a funny look.

"You and Brynn? You mean, you live here?"

"I moved in with Brynn a few months ago when my old roommate got married, and I couldn't find a new place." He peers at me with concern, like I'd suddenly lost my mind. "Didn't Brynn tell you?"

"Nope."

"That's weird."

We stare at each other in silence, and I'm not sure why the news is such a big deal. It's just Ethan. For most of my life, he was like a big brother to me. Okay, that's not true. More accurately, I was like a little sister to *him*. But still, this won't be awkward at all. I'm sure I'll barely even notice he's around.

Wilson shifts his weight, shoving me halfway onto Ethan's lap.

His arm slips around me, keeping me from completely toppling over and face-planting into his wasabi. Even beneath my thick flannel sleeve, the warm pressure of his hand on my upper arm is at once reassuring and dangerously disconcerting. And there's something in his eyes—a glint I've never seen before—that catches me off guard.

I part my lips to say something, anything, but no words come out.

"Q—" he starts, then bites down, flexing his jaw in the same nervous twitch from when we were kids and he had something important to say.

But regrettably, I'm not destined to know what comes next.

In arguably the worst timing in history, the front door flies open.

4

Brynn bursts into the apartment harboring half the snowstorm in her dark, shoulder-length hair. Ethan and I break apart like two teenagers caught making out when they're supposed to be studying.

"I'm so sorry I'm late!" Brynn gushes, unraveling her scarf. "We have a new client who's being audited, and their finances are a mess. Total DEFCON 5 situation."

"You mean DEFCON 1," Ethan corrects, and I can't help noticing he's sitting two feet farther away than before.

"Huh?" Brynn shrugs out of her coat and hangs it on a hook in the foyer.

"DEFCON 5 actually refers to peacetime, whereas DEFCON 1 means nuclear war," he explains. "It's a common misconception perpetuated by film and TV."

"Whatever." Brynn rolls her eyes at him and rushes

over to the couch. Pulling me up from the cushion like a rag doll, she envelops me in a hug so tight, I almost revisit the sushi from five minutes earlier. "I can't believe you're here!"

For a moment, her embrace transports me back in time twenty years, when we were carefree kids playing dress-up with our mothers' high heels and pearls, and all of a sudden, tears sting my eyes. I'd forgotten how much I'd missed her.

"I only wish it hadn't taken me so long," I murmur, realizing I mean every word.

"Me, too," she says, pulling back. Her own eyes are glassy. "But you're here now, and we're going to have the best time. I have the whole weekend planned. And speaking of plans..." She turns to Ethan with an accusatory glare. "Aren't you supposed to be in Atlantic City with your computer nerd friends?"

"If you mean my highly educated and successful college friends from Cornell Tech, then yes."

"Then what are you doing here?"

"We, uh, got kicked out on accusations of card counting," he admits sheepishly.

Brynn crosses her arms in front of her chest, her eyebrows set in a stern frown. "And were you?"

"Dale was testing out the prototype for the Ocular 09X smart glasses to see if they can really predict the probability of hitting twenty-one in blackjack."

"Isn't that just geek-speak for card counting?"

"That's for Dale's lawyer to determine. But probably. For the record," he says, raising his hand like he's being sworn in on the witness stand. "I had no idea. Brice and I don't gamble, so we were at the buffet eating our weight in shrimp. But since our rooms were at the hotel, when Dale got kicked out, rather than look for a new place to stay, it seemed easier to come home. To the apartment. Where I *live*," he said pointedly, casting a glance in my direction.

Now it was Brynn's turn to look sheepish. "Yeah, about that..." She turns to me with the same doe-eyed expression that used to make it impossible for me to stay mad at her when we were kids. "I'm sorry I didn't tell you that Ethan lives with me. But I was worried you'd think we didn't have enough room for you to stay with us, and I didn't want to give you an excuse to change your mind about coming. But... I should have told you."

She looks so earnest and apologetic, I can't help but smile. "It's fine. Honestly. It'll be just like the old days when we used to have sleepovers at your house."

"Uh-uh. No way." Ethan shakes his head. "You're not painting my toenails in my sleep again. I have a guard dog now. Right, Wilson?"

Wilson nuzzles my leg with his head, and I scratch behind his ears. "I don't know about that. He might be my ally now," I say with a laugh.

"Traitor." Ethan makes a face at Wilson, but the gigantic lapdog merely rolls over, offering his stomach for tummy rubs. I happily oblige.

"If he's been disloyal to anyone, it's me." Brynn sinks onto the floor by the couch and snuggles her face in his neck. "You're *my* dog. I named you. But instead of keeping my feet warm at night, you sneak off to Ethan's room, don't you? Don't you?" Her voice is suddenly two octaves higher, and Wilson licks her face, clearly a pro at playing the field.

"Where did his name come from?" I ask, reaching for my hot chocolate.

"Brynn's celebrity crush," Ethan says with a chuckle.

"Owen Wilson?" I hazard a guess.

Ethan only laughs harder, and I glance at Brynn in confusion.

She shoots her brother a playful glower. "I named him after Frank J. Wilson, the accountant who helped catch Al Capone. And for the record," she says, matching Ethan's tone from earlier, "forensic accounting is way sexier than all that *Die Hard*, Jason Bourne nonsense you watch on TV."

"I'll be sure to let Vin Diesel know he should play an accountant in his next action movie role," Ethan teases. "Maybe they can have a harrowing montage with clips of him poring over general ledgers and bank records."

They quibble over the topic for a few more minutes while I listen in amusement. Although they're bantering back and forth, there's no malice in their voices. No condescension. No antagonism of any kind. It's lighthearted and quite sweet, actually.

From the moment they moved three houses down

from ours when I was in the second grade, I'd been fascinated by their family. Their parents reminded me of a couple you'd see on a 1950s sitcom, except instead of sugary sweetness and corny puns, they doled out a healthy dose of playful sarcasm. But the truly remarkable thing—rather than picking on Brynn, Ethan always looked out for her, and then me by extension. On Brynn's first day at school, a clique of mean girls wouldn't let us sit at their lunch table. They were so cruel about it, mercilessly making fun of our clothes and hair, that Brynn started to cry. Ethan—who was three grades older and had already been accepted by the popular crowd—marched right over, put a hand on our shoulders, and led us to join him and his friends. After seeing us eat lunch with fifth graders—and the "cool" kids, no less—no one dared bully us again. That might have been the moment my hopeless crush first began.

"So, what do you two have planned for tomorrow?" Ethan asks, interrupting my trip down memory lane.

"First, we're going shopping," Brynn announces as she reaches for one of the marshmallows. "Then, Quincy has a date." She pops the marshmallow in her mouth, a mischievous glint in her eyes.

"A date?" Ethan chokes on his hot chocolate, and it dribbles down his chin. He wipes it off with the back of his hand. "Didn't you just arrive today?"

"Yes," I say, about to defend myself, but Brynn butts in.

"We arranged it days ago!" she squeals, bouncing on

her heels in her excitement. "I set her up on the new dating app everyone's raving about." Ethan stares blankly, so she explains. "It's called Spin. It was created by the founder of Puzzle Pieces, the dating app your friend Dale used to meet Hannah. It utilizes the same pairing algorithm but has a quirky twist. You know how everyone always goes on a boring first date like drinks or coffee? Well, with this app, once you find a match, you spin this electronic wheel, and it randomly selects an activity for your first date. It's super fun. Like *Wheel of Fortune*, but instead of winning cash, you win love."

Ethan openly scoffs, and I sip my hot chocolate, not wanting to get in the middle of it. To be honest, I think it sounds as ridiculous as Ethan does, but I hate to squelch her enthusiasm. Especially since nine years ago it was her idea to make online dating one of my Christmas Commitments. Though it had been an ill-advised attempt to reconstruct my badly broken heart, I think she's finding personal satisfaction in finally seeing me cross it off the list.

"So, who's the lucky guy?" Ethan asks me.

But once again, Brynn can't help herself. "His name's Sebastian. And he gives off dreamy Clark Kent vibes."

She's positively beaming, and not for the first time, I wonder why Brynn didn't keep him for herself. He seems exactly her type. Tall, lean, and impeccably dressed in a sharp business suit and slicked-back hair with the most even side part I've ever seen. But when I mentioned that they'd make a better match than he and I, she got all squirrelly and evasive on the phone.

"Sebastian?" Ethan raises his eyebrows. "Like the crab in *Little Mermaid*?"

"Did you seriously just bring up a thirty-year-old movie?" Brynn laughs.

"Hey! In my defense, you two sang the soundtrack so relentlessly, I have PTDSD. Post Traumatic Disney Song Disorder. There are still times when 'Part of Your World' gets stuck in my head."

Brynn catches my eye, and we immediately belt out the chorus amid Ethan's loud protests and failed attempts to silence us with marshmallow missiles aimed at our open mouths.

By the time our laughter dissolves, I can't believe I ever doubted my decision to come to New York. In fact, I'm almost sad I'll have to leave in three months. In a matter of hours, I already feel more at home around Brynn and Ethan than I do with my own family. I try not to dwell on the depressing realization.

"In all seriousness," Ethan says, munching on one of the errant missiles. "I hope the date goes well."

"Thanks. Although, there isn't much point, is there? I head back home in three months. So, any relationship I start here is basically doomed."

He chews in silence but seems to be mulling over my words.

"But what if you hit it off?" Brynn asks. "Can't you do long distance?"

"That never works. Besides, I'll be so busy with my new position in the company, I won't even have time for dating."

I toss out the well-rehearsed excuses easily, knowing Brynn wouldn't accept my real reason for remaining single. To this day, I've never told her what Chad said to me all those years ago, the summer we spent in New York. The summer he broke my heart.

And if I'm honest, I don't plan on ever telling her. Or anyone.

5

As I stare up at the whimsical sign for Catnip & Cappuccinos, guilt swirls in my stomach. Considering I'm ten minutes late, poor Sebastian is probably sitting inside waiting for me right now. What if he's hoping to meet his soulmate while, to me, this is nothing more than an opportunity to cross off another task?

I've been so focused on my objective—complete the list and create a winning ad campaign—that I hadn't stopped to consider real people might get hurt in the process.

I smooth back the flyaways disheveled by the chilly gust of wind, reminding myself that it's just one date. Besides, we might not even like each other.

With that thought in mind, I push through the front door.

Once inside the cozy cat café, some of my anxiety

wanes. It's the cutest coffee shop I've ever seen, all bright pops of color and funky, bohemian fabrics. The ruddy brick walls are covered in artwork featuring famous literary cats, from the cheeky Cheshire in *Alice's Adventures in Wonderland* to Dr. Seuss's Cat in the Hat. There are a few less obvious ones, too, like the ginger cat with a smooshed face that I'm pretty sure is supposed to be Crookshanks from *Harry Potter*. As an unabashed booklover, I immediately feel at home.

While I unbutton my new coat—an Isabel Marant shearling jacket I found on sale at Bloomingdale's earlier this morning—my gaze sweeps the café in search of Sebastian.

Cats and kittens in every size and color imaginable canoodle with coffee-sipping patrons, creating a happy, contented aura that spills into every nook and cranny. I can feel my own mouth curling at the edges until a loud sneeze makes me jump, and the smile vanishes.

A man seated in the far corner blows his nose into a napkin, then crumples it into a ball and drops it on the table near a pile of other wadded-up napkins. *Ew.*

My heart plummets when I see his face. Although it's blotchier and rounder than I expected, the man is clearly Sebastian. He retrieves a small lint roller from his briefcase and rubs it furiously over his immaculate navy suit.

The ungracious part of me wants to turn around right now, but it wouldn't be fair to judge him so hastily. Besides, I need to make it through the entire date or else it doesn't count.

"Sebastian?" I say tentatively, approaching the table.

He glances up and smiles. At least, I *think* it's a smile. The chiseled features from his profile photo are now so pink and puffy, he resembles a bloated salmon.

"Quincy, hi. Nice to meet you." He sets the lint roller on the table next to his mountain of soggy napkins. "I hope you don't mind, but I ordered for us while I was waiting."

"No problem. Sorry I'm late." I shrug out of my coat and loop it over the back of the chair before sitting down. "Have you been waiting long?"

"About twenty minutes. I like to arrive ten minutes early. But don't worry, a cute girl like you is worth the wait." His left eye twitches slightly, and I think he's trying to wink, but it's impossible to know for sure. His eyelids are so swollen, they barely budge.

"Welcome to Catnip & Cappuccinos." A young Lucille Ball look-alike wearing a retro-style apron and cat-eye glasses sets two mismatched mugs on the table. "Here are your Persian *Purr*-overs," she says, rolling her *r*'s.

I thank her and reach for the mug, in desperate need of caffeine. And maybe an EpiPen for Sebastian. I'm pretty sure he's having an intense allergic reaction.

"I hope you don't mind, they're decaf," he says,

dumping a sugar packet into his coffee. "My body doesn't react well to caffeine."

"Or to cat dander?" I ask gently, hoping I don't offend him with my concern.

"Is it that obvious?" He sniffles and reaches for the last remaining napkin.

"To be honest, you look like you're pretty miserable. I'd be happy to go somewhere else where you'll be more comfortable."

"No, no, I'm fine. It's only a mild allergy." He blows his nose so loudly the cat being snuggled by a woman seated at the table next to us leaps two feet in the air then lands in her enormous cappuccino, spilling it across the table. The frothy buffet draws half a dozen other cats, triggering a feline feeding frenzy.

"Are you sure? There's a teahouse next door. We could—"

"No, no." He waves his hand, dismissing my offer. "That's not how this works. The app picks the location. If you don't follow the rules, then what's the point of using the app?"

"Um..." I'm not sure what to say. But he's an awfully big stickler for the rules for someone who's basically become one humongous hive.

"Although, I have to say," he adds, casting a displeased glance around the room. "I'm surprised places like this even exist. Aren't all these cats a health code violation?"

"I don't know much about health codes, but cats are

generally considered fairly clean animals. They groom themselves several times a day."

"Yeah, with their *tongues*." He makes a gagging gesture, and I can't help thinking he's being a little uncharitable for someone who's elbow deep in a pile of used tissues.

"So," I say, eager to change the subject. "You're a dog person, then?"

"Not particularly. But they're better than cats. Did you know that people in medieval times believed cats were the devil's minions and escorted souls to Hades?"

"At least they're cute escorts." I smile, trying to lighten the mood as an adorable calico kitten paws at my pant leg. I can't resist bending down to scratch her tiny head, noting the name on her pink collar says Whiskers.

"Cute?" Sebastian scoffs. "Tell that to kids in Iceland. They have a legend called the Yule Cat. The creature prowls the countryside looking for human flesh to devour."

How charming, I think morosely.

"But you won't eat me, will you, Whiskers?" I rub the tip of my finger beneath her chin, and she purrs sweetly. If it weren't for Sebastian, I'd scoop her into my lap.

"If you died alone in your apartment, she'd eat every last appendage, saving your eyeballs for last like a couple of plump maraschino cherries," he says matter-of-factly. "To that little carnivore, you're basically a human charcuterie board."

Is this guy for real? I'm trying to be understanding—after all, his face is starting to look like a lumpy marshmallow slowly expanding to twice its size—but the overt negativity, coupled with the unsavory imagery, is becoming irksome. Still, I can't walk out, no matter how badly I'm tempted. My only hope to put us both out of our misery is to get *him* to end the date. And soon.

"Oh, I don't know about that," I say casually. "My cats are perfectly harmless."

"You have cats?" He gapes at me in horror like I'd just sprouted a tail and whiskers.

"Yep! An even dozen. There's Dasher, Dancer, Prancer, Vixen, Comet, Cupid, Donner, and Blitzen." I tick off the names of my fictitious cats on my fingers, then realize I'm running out of reindeer. In a panic, I add the first names that pop into my mind. "And Justin, Joey, JC, and Lance." As if it isn't bad enough that I'm lying to the man, I embarrassingly rattled off the band members of NSYNC. *Shoot.* Except, I forgot Chris Kirkpatrick. Oh, well. A baker's dozen might have been pushing the bounds of believability.

"I, uh, didn't realize you had so many cats." He shrinks back in his chair and looks as disgusted as if I'd just coughed up a hair ball.

"They're all angels. I think you'll really come to love them. You know, as soon as you get your shots."

"M-my shots?" he stammers.

"Uh-huh," I say brightly. "Weekly shots. In your tushy. But don't worry, you only need to get them for, like, three to five years."

His eyes bulge, and I'm starting to feel a little bad for my charade, but he still hasn't left, so I pull out one last stop.

"What do you think, Whiskers? Do you want Sebastian to be your new daddy?" I lift the adorable kitten into my arms and nuzzle her face.

"I, uh, forgot," Sebastian says quickly, "I promised a friend I'd help him move today."

"Oh, that's too bad." I frown. "Should we reschedule? You can come over to my place and meet the kids."

He must be visualizing a dozen ferocious felines feasting on his lifeless body, because he scoots his chair back so fast it topples over and clatters against the floor. The commotion startles the nearby cats into a hissing hysteria, which sends Sebastian running for the door, wielding his briefcase like a shield.

"Sorry you had to see that, Whiskers." I pat her head. "And I'm afraid I've set a bad example. You shouldn't lie, okay?"

Whiskers licks my hand with her sandpapery tongue, as if to communicate she understands my—admittedly hypocritical—life lesson. She has the most beseeching golden-hued eyes, and as she gazes into mine, I feel a certain kinship with the sweet little thing.

"Whiskers is the last one in her litter to be adopted." The girl who brought our coffee earlier pauses to give the kitten a pitying look. "A couple took her home a few weeks ago, but they brought her back after only one day."

"Oh, how sad." I cuddle Whiskers closer. "How come?"

"They said she wasn't any good at normal cat stuff. She tried to befriend a mouse instead of catching it and wouldn't use the litter box. Oh, and weirdly, they said she'd jump off the furniture but never land on her feet." The girl shrugs and turns away to buss a nearby table.

"Huh." I pet Whiskers's tricolored coat, loving the soft feel of it beneath my fingertips. "That's really not so strange," I say, hoping to comfort her. "And I don't blame you for not using a litter box. It's kind of unsanitary when you think about it."

Whiskers purrs peacefully, snuggling against me. And even though my date is over, and I should be leaving, I don't budge.

Instead, I pull out my phone and dial Brynn.

She answers before the second ring. "Tell me everything!" she squeals. "Was it love at first sight?"

I glance down at Whiskers and smile. "Yeah, I think it was."

6

"Oh, my goodness, they're adorable!" Brynn's friend, Harper Montgomery, gushes as I show her photos of Wilson and Whiskers on my phone.

We're stuffing ourselves with savory crepes and smoked salmon canapés at this eccentric Brunch & Bingo place Brynn loves, which is a surprising combination of elaborately upscale with a dash of down-home diner. She invited Harper, her best friend in New York, to meet us there. I have to admit, when I first laid eyes on the gorgeous and glamorous PR manager, I experienced an unpleasant mix of apprehension, insecurity, and a smidge of envy. The woman practically screams effortlessly cool, from her copper-colored hair cut in an asymmetrical bob to her leopard-print jumper paired with black leather Christian Louboutin ankle boots. Plus, she gets to be Brynn's best friend on a regular basis, in the flesh, whereas I'm merely passing through town. But those are my own issues. Objectively, Harper is great. And I like her even more as she oohs and aahs over each new photo of the humorously large dog and tiny kitten duo, who instantly bonded when I brought Whiskers home last night.

"They really are," Brynn agrees, slurping her Strawberry Sunrise Spritzer through a twisty straw.

We pause the conversation when the bingo caller announces the next number, and we each place a chip on our scorecards.

"When Quincy told me about Whiskers," Brynn continues, "it felt like kismet. I've been meaning to get a friend for Wilson, and he absolutely adores her. He even gives her piggyback rides around the apartment. It's the cutest thing."

"What does Ethan think?" Harper asks, placing another chip on her scorecard.

"Does this answer your question?" I swipe to the photo of Ethan sitting cross-legged on the floor. Wilson had managed to squeeze himself onto Ethan's lap while Whiskers is perched on Ethan's shoulder, both paws on either side of his face like she's trying to give him a hug.

"Wow." Harper whistles. "I didn't think the man could get any sexier, but pair him with a big fluffy dog and adorable kitten and... wow. Can you send me that?" She points to the photo on my phone.

Her request catches me off guard, and I'm not sure

how to respond. Is Harper into Ethan? The thought rattles me more than I care to admit.

"Ew, ew, ew." Brynn covers her ears. "Please stop talking about how sexy my brother is."

"Well, it's your fault for sending me a Christmas card last year. As soon as I saw him in that dorky Rudolph sweater, I knew we were soulmates. And if you'd stop hiding him from me, we could finally start our lives together." She pouts playfully, and I breathe a little easier knowing they haven't actually met. Although, I don't know why I care. Harper seems perfect. Shouldn't I want Ethan to find love with someone as fabulous as Harper?

"My mistake for thinking Aunt Myrtle's hand-knit monstrosity would be adequate repellent," Brynn says with a laugh, then adds in a more serious tone, "I just don't want to think about my brother dating one of my friends. When we go to Sunday brunch and you dish about your romantic first kiss, I don't want to visualize him smooching you."

She shudders at the thought, and suddenly my once-delicious raspberry Danish now tastes like cardboard. I had no idea Brynn felt that way. And again, I have no idea why I care. It isn't as if I have any interest in dating him.

"Fair enough, but don't think I'm giving up hope." Harper takes a bite of a blueberry scone and tosses Brynn a teasing wink. Yet, beneath the easy smiles and playful banter, I sense there's some sincerity in her words.

I quickly change the subject. "How did you and Brynn meet?"

"Oh, that's a funny story!" Harper says brightly. "I handle PR for a few celebrities, and one of my clients got into a bit of a financial scandal."

"*A bit?*" Brynn cries. "It was all over the news!"

"True, but it wasn't her fault. Her money manager did her dirty."

"So, you hired Brynn's firm to clean things up?" I ask.

Harper nods. "We needed *major* damage control, and her firm sends in this reserved, soft-spoken CPA, and I'm about to request a more bullish replacement, but she sits down and starts spouting off numbers and financial strategies I've never even heard of, and, well... I quickly realized the quiet mouse was a bulldog in disguise." Harper laughs. "No one is more passionate about proper money management than our Brynn."

"Numbers are the bedrock of society," Brynn tells us, completely straight-faced.

Harper and I share a smile, then she asks, "What about you two?"

"That's also a funny story," I say with a small chuckle, recalling the memory fondly. "Her family moved into our neighborhood the summer before second grade. I had a lemonade stand at the end of the street, and the day they moved in, Brynn walked over and told me I could make more profit if I had items to upsell. I had no clue what she meant, so she sat down and created an entire business plan in her unicorn notebook. We became partners in the lemonade stand over the rest of the summer, and between her business acumen and my marketing skills, we made enough money to buy matching JanSport backpacks for the first day of school."

"Oh, now that's precious." Harper places a hand to her heart. "I can picture little Brynn now, using a ruler to make a ledger in her notebook to keep track of sales."

Brynn blushes. "Well, if you don't keep track, mistakes can be made!"

"And that's why we love you." Harper squeezes her hand, then says, "I'm jealous you two have been friends for so long. But it must be hard living so far apart."

"It is," we both say in unison.

"Is this your first time visiting Brynn in New York?"

I shift in my seat. "No, but it's been a while."

"A decade," Brynn adds softly, staring at her unfinished crepe, the bingo game forgotten.

Harper's eyes widen in surprise. "But you've seen each other since then?"

"A few times," Brynn says. "When I've gone back home to see my parents. Quincy only visited me once when I was in college."

"Well, you're here now." Harper flashes me a warm smile, as if she senses the underlying tension between us. "Brynn says you're fulfilling some sort of bucket list?"

"Yes," I say simply, suddenly not in the mood to elaborate as I watch Brynn pick at her plate, pushing the same chunk of cantaloupe back and forth through a river of syrup.

I hate to see her upset, but especially when it's because of something I've done... or *haven't* done.

"So, what are some of the items on your list?" Harper asks, single-handedly salvaging our brunch.

"I have to take a dance class," I say, forcing a brightness into my voice, hoping to lighten the mood. "And learn a foreign language."

"Which one?" Harper leans forward with interest.

"Um, I haven't really decided yet."

"Well, let me know when you do. I'm fluent in four languages, so I'd be happy to help you practice, if you choose one I know."

"Wow! Four?" I'm duly impressed. Is there anything this woman *can't* do?

"I guess five, if you count English," she says like it's no big deal. "Plus French, Italian, Spanish, and German."

"That's incredible. How did you learn so many?"

"I picked them up here and there." She gives a nonchalant wave of her hand. "It helped that I lived in Europe for a few years."

"That's so cool. Brynn and I always talked about backpacking through Europe. We even planned a whole route, but then..." I trail off, realizing that was yet another time I'd let her down.

Brynn scoots back her chair. "Excuse me for a sec. I have to use the bathroom."

A silence settles across the table as she leaves, and Harper politely pretends to be enthralled by the pat of butter shaped like a rose.

Hoping to relieve some of the awkward tension, I ask her, "Do you have a bucket list?"

"I used to. I made one in my twenties. But I've since crossed everything off. Now, I have a new list with just one goal on it."

"Oh? And what is it?" I ask, genuinely curious. For such an accomplished woman, I'm guessing it's something seriously impressive like climb Mount Kilimanjaro or dive the Great Barrier Reef.

She scoots closer, her green eyes sparkling, and murmurs in a conspiratorial tone, "Go on a date with Ethan Delaney."

7

The next morning, I open my eyes to find Whiskers coiled in the crook of my neck, purring contentedly. Holding my breath, I slip out of bed, trying not to disturb her, but as soon as my feet touch the floor, she bolts awake and bounces off the edge of the mattress to follow me.

Lacking typical catlike grace, she tumbles to the ground like an action movie stunt double, and I scoop her into my arms. "Are you okay?"

She licks my face, clearly unscathed.

I carry her into the kitchen where I'm hoping to catch Brynn before she leaves for work. She'd returned from the bathroom during brunch yesterday back to her normal self, but I still feel the urge to apologize and offer an explanation, although I'm not sure I have one.

But instead of Brynn, I spot Ethan by the sink, guzzling a glass of water in head-to-toe running gear.

"Morning." He smiles when he sees me, making my stomach do that strange little flutter again.

"You still run?" I ask, recalling his cross-country days.

"Every weekday. Do you?"

I bark out a laugh. "Only if I'm chasing a taco truck."

"That is a worthy reason," he says with a chuckle. "But you should try it sometime. It helps clear my mind in the morning. And if I'm mulling over a problem from the day before, a solution usually pops into my head."

For a moment, I wonder if it would help me come up with a slogan for the energy drink campaign, which has been stubbornly alluding me, but I quickly dismiss the idea. I've loathed running ever since my fifth-grade gym teacher used the mile run as a punishment for the losers whenever we did team sports. Let's just say I've run enough laps to last me a lifetime.

"C'mon, Wilson. Let's go," Ethan calls, grabbing the dog's leash off the hook by the door. "I'm going to take him to use the bathroom before I head out on my run. I tried to take him with me once, but never again. He stopped so many times to sniff things, he gave me whiplash."

The loveable furball bounds down the hall and slides to a stop by Ethan's feet, wagging his entire backside in eagerness. I wish Whiskers would be that excited to use the bathroom. She's had several accidents since I brought her home. I can't for the life of me convince her to use the litter box, not that I blame her.

She wriggles in my arms, and as I glance down at her adorable, entreating face, a thought hits me. "Can we join you?"

He gives me a funny look, like he can't fathom why, but says, "Sure."

I throw on my shearling coat and slip into Brynn's chunky "popping out for a quick coffee" boots and follow Ethan and Wilson to a serene courtyard behind the apartment building. There's a small community garden and a fenced-in dog run, which is where Ethan lets Wilson off his leash.

He happily does his business, and Whiskers continues to squirm in my arms. Curious, I set her down on the grass. She immediately prances after Wilson, and squats to relieve herself behind the same bush.

"Well, that's interesting," Ethan says while I shower Whiskers with praise as she scampers back to me. "Don't most cats use a litter box?"

"Most cats aren't as special as this one." Unabashedly proud, I nuzzle her cheek with the tip of my nose.

When we return to the apartment, the unlikely pair trot into the living room to play with one of Wilson's chew toys.

"You sure you don't want to join me?" Ethan asks, tugging a beanie over his ears. "Central Park is pretty peaceful this early in the morning."

"Thanks, but I signed up for the Big Manhattan Marathon as part of my Christmas Commitments list, so that's enough running for me for the next fifty years or so." I remove the canister of coffee beans from the cupboard, wondering if I can figure out the French press I saw Brynn use yesterday. It made the best coffee I've ever tasted.

Ethan stares at me with a dumbfounded expression. "Wait, that's the first weekend in April, isn't it?"

"Uh-huh."

"And it's a marathon?"

"Yep."

"Which is over twenty-six miles."

"I guess." I shrug, scooping the beans into the burr grinder.

The year I added a marathon to my list, the entire office had decided to participate in the annual LA Marathon, including Matt and Veronica, and I didn't want to be the odd one out. I'd even joined Veronica for a few practice runs, which wound up being my undoing. She found fault with everything I did, from my gait to my posture to the way I sipped my water bottle. She'd even picked apart my running outfit, which—gasp!— wasn't Lululemon, to her great horror.

"Quincy," Ethan says with concern. "You can't run a marathon without training first."

"Why not? I don't want to win or anything. I just need to finish."

"But if you don't train and prepare your body prop- erly, you might injure yourself."

I lean against the counter, considering his words.

He's a runner, so he must know what he's talking about. But he's also the protective older brother type and is probably being overly cautious. "Thanks, but you don't need to worry. I'll be fine."

"Run with me this morning. We'll go two miles, and if you feel fine by the time we finish, I'll stop bugging you about it."

"Only two miles?"

"Yep. Compared to a marathon, two miles should be a piece of cake."

"Okay, fine." I release a heavy sigh, resigning myself to having my coffee afterward. "I guess a couples miles won't kill me."

As I lag behind Ethan several minutes later, I'm ready to eat my words. There's a stabbing pain in my side, and my lungs are no longer transporting oxygen to the rest of my body. And not to be overdramatic, but I'm fairly certain I'm about to die.

"How's it going?" Ethan calls over his shoulder.

"Delightful," I grunt, shooting daggers at his back. The man doesn't even have the decency to break a sweat. "How much farther?" The question barely makes it past my labored wheezing, and I'm pretty sure the extra effort to speak just depleted my remaining oxygen because I'm starting to feel light-headed.

"About a mile."

His words sound like a death sentence, and I don't think I'll last another few feet, let alone an entire mile. "Okay, you've made your point," I gasp, creating a puff of white in the frigid air. "If I'm going to run a marathon, I need to train."

He jogs backward until we're running side by side. "Good thing you have the best trainer in New York."

"You must really like torturing people."

"Nah, just you." He flashes me a heart-stopping grin, and I stumble over my own feet.

His hand juts out to catch me, and I try to ignore the quiver in my stomach when his gloved fingers wrap around my arm.

"First lesson: slow down. You're pushing yourself too hard. It's okay to start at an easier pace." He leads by example, and I adjust my stride to match his, immediately feeling some relief.

"Now," he continues, "try to steady your breath. Inhale deeply, hold for a few seconds, then exhale in a controlled release."

I try to do as he says. The first few breaths are still onerous and ragged, but eventually, I find a rhythm and notice some of the cramping subside.

"Lastly," he says, "keep your chest high and look around you. Focus on the environment rather than the weight of your feet or the strain in your muscles."

For the first time, I take in my surroundings, and I'm stunned by what I see. Early morning light hangs like a golden halo over the snow-dappled trees, and mist rises off the frosted ground, lending an otherworldly aura to the picturesque scenery. I've seen Central Park before, but never like this. And never so devoid of people, so peaceful, so quiet. It's devastatingly lovely, like a wintry paradise made for two, and my heart swells with wonder at how such an unexpected oasis could exist in a bustling metropolis like Manhattan.

For a moment, I've forgotten all about the ache in my side and the lead weights I'm convinced someone hid in my shoes, and I'm reminded why I fell in love with New York City all those years ago, why I'd wanted to move here with Brynn. The word *magical* may sound cliché, but there's an undeniable truth to the description. New York ignites your imagination; makes you believe anything is possible. At least, it did once....

Perhaps, after all this time, I could learn to love this city again. But as we round a corner, and a familiar landmark comes into view, my heart stops.

The iconic Gapstow Bridge looms ahead, hauntingly beautiful. The stalwart stone arch stretches across the hazy pond, a rustic contrast to the ritzy Midtown Manhattan skyline beyond. Although it's traditionally recognized as a popular spot for proposals, my experience with the most romantic location in Central Park couldn't be more opposite.

It isn't until Ethan glances over his shoulder and asks, "Are you okay?" that I realize I've stopped moving.

"Uh-huh." I nod slowly, my thoughts a tangled web of unwelcome memories.

There are many moments you can run from in life—embarrassments, regrets, and failures—but others cling to you forever, seeping into your very being, becoming a transformative part of your soul.

For me, that moment occurred on the Gapstow Bridge.

A moment I'll never forget.

8

Over the next few weeks, I slowly settle into my new life in New York. Runs with Ethan become easier—almost enjoyable, even. And while I still haven't devised a winning ad campaign, I try not to stress about it, trusting that it'll come to me eventually. Besides, it's a moot point if I don't finish everything on my list.

So far, I've checked off three tasks: move to New York, online dating, and learn to knit. Brynn actually took up the hobby with me, and we've spent several evenings in front of the fireplace knitting scarves and swooning over Colin Firth in the BBC's episodic production of *Pride and Prejudice*.

Although, I use the term *scarf* loosely. Brynn's turned out fantastic—she somehow mastered a complicated diamond pattern on her first try—while my simpler attempt resembles a tangled fisherman's net.

Still, I technically know *how* to knit, even if I'm not any good at it. Plus, my efforts weren't in vain. Whiskers has adopted my sorry excuse for a scarf as her new toy, and she and Wilson often play an extremely lopsided game of tug-of-war, which ultimately results in Wilson towing her around the apartment while she clings to one end like a water skier.

Some nights, when we're really lucky, Ethan reads aloud to us from *The Great Gatsby* while we knit. His voice is strong and soothing, yet there's something about his inflection—the passion in his voice, perhaps —that brings the story to life just like when we were kids. Back then, Brynn and I would pester him until he relented and lulled us to sleep with *The Adventures of Huckleberry Finn* and *The Boxcar Children*.

At first, I thought it might be strange to live with Ethan, especially since we both work from home—he builds ecommerce websites—and we wind up spending a good chunk of the day together, from chatting over morning coffee after our runs to coordinating our lunch breaks. But now, I can't imagine what my time in New York would be like without him.

And yes, occasionally my stomach still flip-flops whenever his hand accidentally grazes mine or when he flashes one of his sexy, slanted smiles. But I've come to accept it, like an inconvenient bout of indigestion, and it in no way encumbers our friendship. He's still Ethan Delaney, my best friend's brother, and a man with whom I have zero romantic future.

Which is why when Harper insists we all join her at some jazz lounge to celebrate my first month in New York, I only hesitate for half a second.

Sure, the invitation might be an excuse for her to finally meet Ethan and charm him into falling madly in love with her. But so what if it is? They could very well be soulmates, and who am I to stand in the way of true love?

I repeat the sentiment to myself several times as the muscled bouncer waves Brynn, Ethan, and me into the dimly lit lounge. Like Harper, the space is sleek, sophisticated, and trendy without trying too hard. Dark-stained wood, leather, and steely metal blend with soft, sumptuous fabrics in vibrant reds and purples, creating a sultry atmosphere that's the perfect complement to the seductive sounds emanating from the stage.

Ethan places a hand on my lower back and guides me through the milling crowd. The gesture, though innocent and utilitarian in purpose, sends a shiver across my skin, and I try not to concentrate on the woodsy scent of his body wash or how handsome he looks in a simple wool coat.

My gaze keeps traveling to the stubble on his jawline, so I purposefully redirect it straight ahead, searching for Harper. When I spot her in a booth near the stage, my step falters slightly. She looks absolutely stunning. Her flawless skin glows in a burgundy off-the-shoulder sweater, and her impossibly long legs are crossed beneath the table, shown off to alluring effect by snug leather pants.

I'm suddenly glad I swapped out my boring beige cardigan—even if it is cashmere—for the indigo silk blouse that enhances the blue of my eyes, then scold myself for the trivial thought.

Harper smiles and waves when she sees us, and I notice there's a man seated in the booth beside her. An incredibly attractive man, who could easily be the star of a Spanish soap opera. The rakish rogue the heroines have a duel to the death over before realizing he has a twin and they're actually each in love with a different brother.

I breathe a little easier realizing Harper must have given up on her one life goal of enchanting Ethan, since she clearly brought a date.

"I'm so glad you guys could make it!" Harper beams when we reach the table. "Quincy, sit here, by me." She pats the cushion next to her, and I remove my coat before sitting down.

Since there's no more room on this side, Ethan sits across from us, and Brynn follows.

"Well, isn't this cozy?" Harper says as we settle in. "Everyone, this is my friend Javier. Javier, this is Quincy, who I've been telling you about, and this is Brynn, and you must be Brynn's elusive brother, Ethan." She extends her hand to him gracefully, and for some reason, I hold my breath while they greet each other. I suppose I'm waiting for a spark to ricochet off their fingertips, like the moment in every romantic comedy when you know it's love at first sight. But Ethan's expression doesn't reveal any emotion beyond casual friendliness.

"It's a pleasure to meet you all." Javier's voice is deep and velvety, and although he speaks in the plural, his full attention is directed at me. There's something in his smile—a glimmer of open interest—that makes me uneasy, especially with Harper sitting between us.

After a few minutes of chitchat, she asks me to let her out of the booth so she can order a bottle of champagne at the bar, and wrangles Brynn to help carry the glasses.

As I'm left alone with Ethan and Javier, I notice a strange energy rippling across the table. The two men are eyeing each other, as though sizing up the competition. Is Ethan jealous of Harper's date? My stomach sinks with disappointment, but I remind myself that I don't care.

"So, Javier, how do you and Harper know each other?" Ethan asks, confirming my suspicion.

"We work at the same PR firm. She mostly handles actors, while I work with musicians. Wes is a client." He nods toward the stage.

The young man pouring his heart and soul into the microphone reminds me a little of the jazz greats Ray Charles and Louis Armstrong mixed with modern influences. His raspy baritone is achingly beautiful. The kind of music you feel all the way to your core.

"You're lucky," I say. "He's incredibly talented."

"I couldn't agree more." Javier smiles at me again, the same intimate smile that makes me squirm. I glance over my shoulder to gauge Harper's progress at the bar, but I can't see her through the sea of people.

"So, Quincy." Javier drapes his arm across the back of the booth, angling his body to face me—his noticeably fit body. The satiny fabric of his pin-striped button-down strains slightly across his broad chest. "Harper tells me you're on a quest to complete a bucket list?"

"I am. Only seven more tasks to go."

"And what's next?"

"Well, I can technically complete them in any order, but if I'm going chronologically..." I pause a moment to conjure the list in my mind, then say, "Next, I have to learn to play a musical instrument."

"Really?" Javier's dark eyes light up. "That's right in my wheelhouse. I don't play an instrument myself, but I'm surrounded by the world's most talented musicians." He motions toward the stage with a sweeping gesture, and I have to agree. The collective talent is seriously impressive. From the saxophone to the clarinet to the piano, each instrument appears to be an extension of the artists, as though they each exist to perform this one song, in this one moment. I've seen my share of live performances and can tell when someone is born to play.

"Which instrument do you want to learn?" Javier asks.

"Honestly, I haven't decided. Most likely whichever is the easiest. I'm not musically gifted."

"I doubt that," Javier says. "I bet you excel at anything you put your mind to."

"That's very kind of you to say." I force a smile. Although well-meant, I've never appreciated that particular sentiment. It implies that the only thing standing between a person and success is effort. But that isn't always true, is it?

Javier continues to smile at me, as if he finds even my silence fascinating.

Ethan makes this weird cough-like throat-clearing sound, and the annoyance in his gaze is unmistakable. He's probably irritated on Harper's behalf. But I don't think Javier is actually flirting with me. He's just being friendly.

"I'll tell you what." Javier pulls his wallet out of his back pocket and removes a business card. "Let's exchange numbers. I'll arrange a lesson with one of my musicians."

"Oh, I couldn't ask you to do that," I say quickly, shooting Ethan a glance I'm hoping communicates, *Calm down, I'm not trying to highjack Harper's date*, so he can wipe the indignant look off his face.

"You're not asking, I'm offering. Actually I'm insisting. And trust me, the guys will be fighting over the opportunity. Who could resist giving a private lesson to a beautiful woman such as yourself?"

My cheeks are burning now, and although I'm

avoiding Ethan's gaze, I feel his disapproval radiating across the table. But there's no way Javier is on a date with Harper—perfection personified—and has decided to hit on me. He's simply being nice to one of her friends. "I, uh, don't have a business card." Even if his offer is harmless, I don't plan on taking him up on it. It would be too weird.

"Here," he says, retrieving his cell phone from the breast pocket of his sports coat. "Program your number, and I'll give you a call when I set something up."

I hold the phone in my hand, unsure what to do. I'm convinced Javier is merely being magnanimous, but something about it still doesn't feel right. And Ethan's critical glare isn't helping.

Luckily, Brynn and Harper return from the bar in the nick of time, carrying a bottle of Dom Pérignon and five glasses. At the last second, Harper quickens her step ever so slightly so she reaches the table first.

"Sorry we took so long, the bar is packed." She sidles into the booth beside Ethan, and hands him the bottle of bubbly with a smile that's equally effervescent.

"No worries," Javier says breezily, shifting a smidge closer, his arm still draped behind me. I get a strong whiff of his spicy cologne. "We were just getting to know each other."

"Excellent!" Harper's gaze briefly flickers between me and Javier before she fixes her dazzling grin on Ethan. "Then let's continue, shall we?"

Suddenly, reality hits me like a projectile champagne cork to the forehead, and I feel like the densest person in the world. This was her plan all along, wasn't it? Operation Land a Date with Ethan Delaney is in full swing.

Which means Javier isn't *her* date... he's *mine*.

9

"So, Javier seems nice." Brynn wiggles her eyebrows over the brim of her mug, both elbows propped on the smooth marble of the kitchen island.

"Uh-huh," I murmur noncommittally and take a sip of coffee.

"You don't think he's too... slick?" Ethan slides fresh-off-the-griddle pancakes onto each of our plates, steam still curling from the delicately golden crusts.

Between the three of us, he's the only one who can cook, and makes a habit of fixing a humongous breakfast every Saturday, which Brynn and I eagerly devour.

"If by slick you mean ridiculously handsome, charming, and successful, then yes." She spins on her barstool to face me. "What do you think, Quince?"

"I think..." I take another sip of coffee then hop off the stool. "I think I need a refill."

Brynn groans. "Quit avoiding the question. And please tell me you gave him your number."

Ethan casts me a curious glance, and I look away, my attention focused on the aromatic Colombian roast filling my mug. "I did."

Brynn squeals, so I feel the need to add, "But only because he offered to arrange a music lesson, and Harper insisted I accept the favor, so don't get any ideas."

"We'll see." She grins, and there's something about the way she swivels on the barstool, her legs swinging, that reminds me of when we were little girls.

We used to tease each other about our Hollywood crushes. She fangirled over Orlando Bloom whereas I pretended to daydream about Chad Michael Murray rather than admit the real object of my infatuation. And now that I know how she feels about friends pining over her brother, I'm glad I kept it a secret.

While we're on the topic of Javier, I'm tempted to ask Ethan about Harper. They seemed to hit it off, although I'm not sure if they exchanged phone numbers. But if they did, do I really want to know?

Deciding to change the subject, I ask Brynn, "Are you ready for our art class today?"

"Do you mind if we reschedule?" Her tone is apologetic as she explains, "A coworker asked if I'd help him out at the office for a few hours. He's stuck sorting piles of crumpled receipts for a client, and I feel bad for him."

"Not at all. Next weekend is fine." I sip my coffee,

intrigued by her sudden fascination with the label on the maple syrup bottle.

I honestly don't mind postponing. It's a free, low commitment paint-in-the-park class being taught by art students every Saturday. And I can just as easily check it off my Christmas Commitments list next week. At the moment, I'm much more interested in the blush dappling Brynn's cheeks.

"So, this coworker… does he have a name?" I prod.

"Of course he does." She grabs her knife and fork and starts cutting her remaining pancake in an even grid. "Doesn't everybody?"

"And would you care to share it?"

She shoves a forkful of pancake into her mouth, then mumbles, knowing full well we can't understand a word she's saying. I'd be annoyed, except I evaded her string of questions not five minutes earlier.

"Is it Oliver?" Ethan asks, scooping the last pancake onto his own plate.

Brynn gags on her massive mouthful and gulps her orange juice until she can breathe again.

"Who's Oliver?" I ask. "And why does the name sound so familiar?"

"Because he's the coworker Brynn's always talking about. I think she's into him," Ethan says.

"I am not!" Brynn protests a little too adamantly.

"Then why does your face get all red whenever his name comes up?" Ethan brandishes his fork like a laser pointer, drawing attention to her heated complexion.

"It doesn't." She presses both hands to her flushed cheeks, but she's not fooling anyone.

"I don't know, Brynn," I say with a teasing smile. "Ethan has a point. I think you might like this guy."

"Well, you're both wrong. And I have to get to work." She slides off the stool with a huff.

"And see Oliver?" I playfully purse my lips into a kissy face.

Brynn rolls her eyes as she sets her plate in the sink, but her fair skin is flaming. "Aren't you both adults?"

"Do I have to come down to your office and demand to know his intentions toward you?" Ethan asks, ignoring her rhetorical question.

"He doesn't have any intentions. We're just friends." Brynn shrugs on her coat. "Unlike Javier, who's made his intentions toward Quincy *very* clear."

That sufficiently silences us both, and she throws one end of her scarf over her shoulder with a triumphant flourish before gliding outside.

An uncomfortable silence permeates the kitchen, only disrupted by the background noises of Wilson and Whiskers roughhousing in the living room. And by roughhousing, I mean Wilson lies on his back and lets Whiskers pounce on him while he pretends to swat her away.

I flip open my laptop, then—purely for the sake of filling the void—say out loud, "Since we aren't going to the art class until tomorrow, I guess I should finally settle on which language I want to learn. I'm wavering between French and Italian."

"What about coding?"

"You mean like computer programing?" I ask. "I've never thought of coding as a language."

"You sound like my high school Spanish teacher. I tried to convince her that coding should count toward foreign language credit."

"And did you?"

"Not even close. But it's definitely a language. When the computers take over the world, coders will be the only ones who can communicate with our evil overlords."

"You may have a point. And I admit, I do find the concept intriguing."

"I can teach you, if you want."

"Thanks, but absolutely not. You're already doing too much by letting me intrude on your morning runs. I couldn't ask you to be my tutor as well as my trainer."

"You're not asking." The corner of his mouth curls into a mischievous grin as he adds, "I'm offering. Actually, I'm *insisting*." He matches Javier's inflection from last night perfectly, and I blush before I can stop myself.

"Are you sure?"

"Positive. I can use an excuse to leave these dirty dishes for later." Tossing me a grin, he sets his plate in the sink on top of Brynn's. "I can teach you how to build a website."

"A website for what?"

He pauses a moment to consider my question. "The simplest would probably be a blog."

"A blog?" I wrinkle my nose. "My life is boring. What do I have to blog about?"

"Oh, I don't know," he says with an air of sarcasm. "How about your crazy competition and list of Christmas Commitments?"

"*Crazy*, huh?" I arch an eyebrow, amused.

"Sorry. That's crass. I meant to say bonkers. Nutty. Wacky. Cuckoo. Loony—"

"Okay, okay," I laugh. "You made your point, Mr. Thesaurus. I guess it would be nice to have a journal to look back on. But I don't exactly want other people to see it."

"Not a problem. We can make it private. Only you will have access. Well, and me."

"And you won't read it?"

"Did I read your Nancy Drew diary when we were kids?"

"I don't know, did you?" I ask, mortified at the thought. But how else would he know it had Nancy Drew on the cover?

"Matt found it hidden in the tree house, and I made him put it back. And if he didn't, I threatened to tell the entire school he had a crush on Mrs. Gregors."

"The school nurse?" I shriek. "She was like a hundred years old!"

"Only eighty-seven, but still. It wouldn't have

looked good. So I was confident your innermost secrets were safe."

"Then I guess you can be trusted." I smile, marveling at how he looked out for me, even when I didn't know it.

As I follow Ethan to his bedroom, a mixture of curiosity and timidity settles in my stomach. There's something oddly vulnerable about stepping inside the space where someone sleeps. A person's room is an extension of themselves, an intimate glimpse into who they are.

Although it's roughly the same size as the guest room, Ethan's bedroom boasts a better view of Central Park. And rather than light, creamy neutrals, the decor is dominated by grays and dark blues. Framed vintage *Star Wars* posters, artsy black-and-white photographs of the Brooklyn Bridge, and overflowing bookshelves cover the walls. It's all... so Ethan. Eclectic and a little bit unexpected but also perfect, like you couldn't imagine it any other way. The room even smells like him, manly and delicious and wholly distracting.

"Q, you can sit down." Ethan taps the back of the chair beside him, and I realize I've been hovering in the doorway.

I tear my gaze from his unmade bed—the rumpled, silvery sheets that look buttery soft—and join him at his desk. The cluttered workspace is long and modern with a transparent tabletop, and three enormous computer monitors partially block the large picture window framing the cityscape.

He taps the keyboard, and the center monitor springs to life, revealing one of the coolest websites I've ever seen. The words *MAD Market* sprawl across the top of the screen in a unique, eye-catching font that perfectly complements the bold, fresh design. It appears to be an online store of some kind, and I immediately want to buy the luxurious-looking organic cotton robe featured prominently on the page.

But before I can see the price, Ethan closes out the screen.

"Hey! I was looking at that," I protest, reaching over him to grab the mouse.

He slides it out of reach. "It isn't finished yet."

"Wait." I lean back in surprise. "This is one of *your* websites?"

"It's a small side project." He fiddles with the mouse, deftly avoiding my gaze as he opens a blank tab.

"It didn't look like a small side project," I say, watching him closely. He seems twitchy—nervous, almost—which is so unlike him. "Can I see it?"

"It's nothing. We should get to work if you—"

I place my hand over his, stilling his fingers, and his voice falls away.

We both stare at our stacked hands, neither of us moving. His skin is warm, and heat spreads through my fingertips to my palm, traveling the length of my arm, scattering goose bumps along the way.

Startled by the sensation, I yank my hand away and take a moment to untangle my muddled emotions. "You don't have to show me if you don't want to," I say in the kind of soft, tentative voice you'd use to avoid spooking a skittish horse. "But it's definitely not nothing. And I'd genuinely love to see it. One day. When you're comfortable sharing it."

He thoughtfully strokes the mouse, then, with a quick click, the site reappears. "It's not finished yet," he reiterates, still avoiding my gaze. "It's a passion project I've been working on for the last year or so."

"Is it an online marketplace?" I ask, noting the various product categories.

"Yeah, like the one that's already taken over the world," he says wryly, as if even he can't believe he's trying to compete with such a monolithic company. "Except all the products on my site are heavily curated from businesses with a shared ethos to protect people and the planet as much as possible."

I nod as I scroll, recognizing several B Corp, fair trade, and cruelty-free brands I already buy.

"The acronym MAD stands for Make A Difference. Anytime you need something, like a new frying pan, for example, you can type it into the search bar or use the category filters. All the products that pop up have been carefully vetted, so you can be assured each purchase you make is from a company making a positive impact on the world."

As I surf the site, I can tell he's put a lot of

thought, time, and effort into the project. It's stylish yet streamlined. User-friendly and functional yet high-end. In short, it's brilliant, and my chest swells with pride. "Ethan, this is incredible. Seriously. I'd definitely use this as my main hub for online shopping. The idea is so ingenious, I can't believe no one has done it before."

If I'm not mistaken, there's a faint flush beneath his five-o'clock shadow. Is Ethan Delaney blushing? I can't believe it. There's also this adorable glow of appreciation in his hazel eyes. And maybe something more, something deeper, but I can't quite place it.

He clears his throat and looks away, staring at the screen. "There are a few others, but they're operating on a much smaller scale. I don't think anyone's crazy enough to take on the top dog."

"That's because they're not a Daft Delaney," I say with a laugh, recalling the tongue-in-cheek idiom Ethan and Brynn's dad always used whenever they had an ambitious or outlandish idea.

The Delaneys lived by a completely different life philosophy than the Carmichaels. In my family, you either succeeded or you might as well not even try. But in Ethan's family, every failure was a step forward. "When does your site go live?"

"Honestly? Probably never."

"What? Why?"

Ethan combs his fingers through his hair, his telltale sign of frustration. "I've hit a wall. In order for this idea to have a shot, it needs momentum. It needs money. Serious money."

"Like investors?"

"Yeah. And a killer marketing campaign. No one can use the site if they don't know it exists."

He has a point, and my heart sinks. "It's not like a Delaney to give up."

"Tell me about it." He grins ruefully. "But I'm man enough to admit when I'm in over my head."

I can't help thinking it's a funny choice of words. In all my life, I've never heard Dad or Matt say they couldn't do something. Heaven forbid they ever ask for help.

"What if I help?" I blurt.

"What do you mean?"

"Well, marketing is kind of my thing. What if I help you put together a presentation for investors?"

He shakes his head. "I couldn't let you do that, Q. You've got a lot on your plate already. Between completing your list and the energy drink campaign, you don't have time to do me a favor. Especially one this big."

"Yes, I do. Besides, you and Brynn have done so much for me, and this is the only thing I have to offer in return. Please, let me do this. I really want to help." I press my palms together, earnestly pleading my case, and I think it's starting to work.

Ethan's features soften. "You're sure?"

"One thousand percent." I dig my phone out of my

pocket. "I'll take a few notes and start brainstorming this afternoon."

I pull up the Notes app, eager to get started, but my pulse lurches as he gently rests his hand on my forearm. My throat goes dry when I meet his gaze. He's looking at me with such tenderness, I suddenly forget how to breathe.

"Thanks, Q. It means a lot to me." His voice is thick and soft like a well-loved blanket when he adds, "And you have more to offer than you think."

I mumble something incoherent, too flustered to form words.

For what feels like forever, neither of us moves.

A strange energy sizzles between us.

The room feels hot, and I wet my lips.

Ethan inches forward, a mere breath away.

Then my phone buzzes in my hand.

We both glance at the screen.

It's a text from Javier.

10

"It's from Javier," I say unnecessarily. "Do you remember Wes, the musician who performed last night?"

"Sure. He was great."

"Apparently, he's offered to teach me the conga drum." I still can't believe it. Even though Javier said he'd arrange a lesson, I didn't think it would actually happen.

"That's amazing, Q. What a cool opportunity."

"The thing is..." I trail off, rereading the text to make sure. "He says it would have to be this afternoon." I glance from Ethan to the computer screen, then back to my phone, feeling torn.

"Go. We can do this anytime." He smiles, but I notice it doesn't quite reach his eyes.

Part of me wants to stay and explore whatever almost happened between us. But the other part of me

—the smarter, more sensible one—knows I need to extricate myself from the situation, and that whatever did or *didn't* happen is best forgotten.

"Thanks." An emptiness creeps over me as I text Javier back, like I'd just closed the door on something potentially life-altering. But even having the thought makes me feel foolish. I'm infusing more meaning into the moment than I should. Time for a much-needed reality check.

"Well," I say awkwardly, rising to my feet. "Guess I'd better get ready. Javier will be picking me up soon."

"Have a good time." Ethan turns back to the computer, as if he's silently releasing me from any lingering obligation I might have to stay.

My conflicted emotions weigh down my movements as I freshen up my hair and add a touch of mascara and matte lipstick.

I'd asked Javier to pick me up at the curb, and when he sends a text letting me know his car is out front, I give Whiskers a quick kiss goodbye before slipping outside. For some reason, I'm grateful Ethan is still in his room and doesn't see me leave.

When I step into the crisp, wintry air, I tug my Burberry scarf tighter around my neck to block out the cold and look toward the street.

Javier leans against a black town car with all the casual elegance of a cover model. And in his sleek onyx suit and calf-length wool coat, he could very easily be one.

He straightens when he sees me, and his entire face brightens in a near-blinding smile. How on earth does someone get their teeth so white? It doesn't seem humanly possible.

"Quincy! It's great to see you again. I'm so glad the timing worked out." To my surprise, he greets me with a light kiss on each cheek, feathery soft and subtly seductive in a way only he could pull off. His cologne—which reminds me of the spiced bourbon my dad reserves for special occasions—lingers as he opens the car door and ushers me into the back seat.

"Me, too. Thanks so much for arranging this." I settle on the creamy leather seat, impressed by the pristine interior. Not only is the upholstery smooth instead of sticky, but there isn't a single moldy food wrapper or stale wad of gum to be seen. I bet I could swipe a fingertip over the cupholder wearing a white glove and not find a trace of dust. So unlike my first experience in a New York cab.

"You look gorgeous, by the way," Javier adds as he climbs in next to me. Normally, his remark would make me uncomfortable. But there's something about the way he delivers the compliment that makes it sound mundane, like he overuses the word the way some people say they just ate the most *gorgeous* tuna fish sandwich or how they found the most *gorgeous* parking spot.

I glance out the window toward Ethan's window. Ethan, who never gives flippant flattery. But when he does say something nice, it feels personal, measured, and thoughtful. And you know he means every word. For a split second, I wish he were looking down, watching us. But he's not. And why would he?

I direct my attention back to Javier. "Thanks." I twist my restless hands in my lap, suddenly wondering if I should have given this excursion a bit more thought. Even though Harper vouched for him, I barely know Javier, and I've never even met Wes. Now I'm going to embarrass myself in front of two virtual strangers.

The closer we get to the recording studio, the clearer it becomes that I was swept away by the idea of learning from a famous musician without considering all the implications. Like my inevitable humiliation.

By the time we step into the sound booth, I'm practically vibrating with nerves. And it doesn't help that Wes is even more intimidating in person than he was on stage. He's well over six feet of solid muscle and has the kind of flawless dark skin that makes it impossible to determine his age. I'm going to guess somewhere in his thirties, give or take ten years.

"You must be Quincy." Wes smiles at me, and the second his lips tilt upward, my anxiety melts away. It's the type of smile that not only reaches his eyes, but radiates from every pore, like he's lit from within. I instantly feel like I've made a new friend.

"Thank you so much for doing this. I'll try not to be too much of a burden on your time."

"No burden," he says with a wave of his hand.

"Music is my passion. I welcome any and every oppor-tunity to introduce someone to something I love."

I smile at his infectious sincerity. "I'm glad you feel that way because I'm afraid you have your work cut out for you. I have zero musical ability."

"Everyone has music inside them." He taps his chest, right above his heart. "We simply have to let it out."

"Well, my music is buried pretty deep. Like in one of those bunkers built for the apocalypse."

Wes and Javier laugh, not realizing it wasn't a joke. I don't even sing in the shower anymore. Not since my neighbor called the cops when she mistook my Mariah Carey impersonation as a cry for help.

"Good thing I like a challenge," Wes says, adding, "And the conga will be perfect for you. There are no keys or strings to learn. It's merely a vessel to channel your inner song."

I nod like I understand what he's saying, but in actuality it sounds like woo-woo gibberish to me.

Javier wishes us luck and excuses himself to join a heavyset man seated on the opposite side of the lami-nated glass, and once again, I'm reminded that my epic failure will have an audience. I loosen my scarf.

"Make yourself comfortable." Wes gestures to a squat stool beside what I'm assuming is the conga drum —it looks a little like a small, skinny wine barrel with worn leather stretched over the top. And judging from the knicks and divots in the aged wood, it could easily be a hundred years old. Not exactly what I was expecting.

"To be honest," I say, stiffly lowering myself onto the stool, "the only thing that might make me feel a little more comfortable is Prozac."

He releases another laugh, and much like his singing voice, the sound is thick and warm, and wraps around me like a soft wool sweater. "Trust me, music is much more cathartic than medicine." He settles on a larger stool beside me, a modern-looking drum propped between his knees. He nods to the man in the control room, who moves some knobs and switches on the console, and slow, sultry jazz music spills into the confined space.

With his gaze fixed on me, Wes beats the drum in perfect tempo, making it look effortless, almost second nature.

I stare back, completely at a loss. Has our lesson started? Because I have no clue what I'm doing.

"Don't overthink it," Wes says, sensing my hesitation. "Place your hands on the drum and let the rhythm find you."

Let the rhythm find you? Is this guy for real? I'm starting to feel a little salty toward my musical Yoda, who insists on speaking in vague adages, but it's too late to back out now. For some reason, I swing and stretch my arms like I'm preparing for a triple backflip before placing my palms on the drum.

The surface is silky smooth, and as I run my fingertips across it, tingles skitter up my arms.

"Close your eyes," Wes instructs. "Then allow your hands to move when and how they want. Don't worry about what it sounds like. Focus on what it *feels* like."

I want to tell him it feels awkward and unnatural, but I refrain. He's doing me a favor, so I might as well play along. Besides, I just need to get through the lesson and get Wes's stamp of approval so I can check the task off my list.

Taking a deep breath, I close my eyes and let the melody wash over me, trying to pinpoint a discernible cadence I can mimic. I give the drum a couple tentative taps, wincing at how clumsy they sound. Frustration builds in my chest, heightened by my regret. I should never have agreed to this.

My thoughts drift to the first time I played the violin in front of my family. They'd all gathered in the living room, while I stood in front of the hearth, framed by the ornate mantel, a picture of hopeful naivety at the tender age of twelve. I'd been taking lessons for months and looked forward to finally unveiling all my hard work.

Thanks to my nerves, the first few notes debuted as ear-splitting screeches. Matt and Veronica snickered, but I plowed ahead, performing a rendition of "Amazing Grace" that made the neighbor's dog howl for relief. Needless to say, my siblings weren't very gracious after that. But their unrestrained laughter didn't compare to the pitying looks of disappointment splashed across my parents' faces.

Don't get me wrong, they'd tried to spare my feelings. They'd immediately shushed the snickering and tried to hide their dismay behind smiles of encouragement, but I could see it in their eyes. Something had gone awry when I was born, as if Matt and Veronica had monopolized all the prime genetic material, leaving me with the dregs, and everyone knew it.

The painful memory must have registered on my face, because Wes says softly, "Music has always been a balm to the downtrodden; a way to communicate when you have no voice, to transform the pain into something beautiful, something worthwhile."

As he speaks, I barely notice that my hands are still moving, tapping the drum of their own accord.

"The conga has roots in Afro-Cuban culture," he continues, my hands drumming along as I listen. "When thousands of slaves were brought to Cuba from the Bantu-speaking Congo region of Africa during the seventeenth and eighteenth centuries, they brought their music with them. Because music comes from a person's heart, from their soul, it's not something that can be stolen or stripped away. And in its purest form, it's not about performance or perfection. It's personal."

Something in his story unlocks a hidden compartment inside of me, where there isn't this constant fear that no matter what I do or how hard I try, I'll never be good enough.

My hands are flying across the drum now, and I have no idea what it sounds like, but I know I've never felt this free, this unencumbered by expectations I'll never meet. And it feels incredible.

We continue in this state of bliss for several songs, and when our jam session finally comes to an end, my cheeks are flushed and a little sore from smiling so wide.

Wes is smiling, too. "I'm pleased to say that you, Quincy Carmichael, have successfully learned the conga." He stands and offers his hand in congratulations, but I fling my arms around his waist instead.

"Thank you, thank you," I murmur as I hug the giant man within an inch of his life.

He chuckles. "It was my pleasure." When I release him, he lifts the battered but beautiful conga off the ground, and lovingly pats its side. "This ol' girl has been with me a long time. I played my first song on her, and my father before me."

I'm moved beyond words that he'd allow me to use a family heirloom, and even more amazed when he holds it out to me. "I'd like you to keep her."

"Oh, wow," I stammer, too stunned for words. "Th-that's incredibly generous of you, but I couldn't possibly accept."

"I'd like her to go where she's needed most. I barely have time to play her anymore, and I have a feeling she'll be happier with you, freeing more of the music locked inside of you."

I can't help but smile at the endearing way he speaks about an inanimate object. And if I'm honest, I'm starting to buy into all the woo-woo sentimentality. Besides, maybe it would be good for me to have a little more music in my life.

"I can't thank you enough, Wes," I say as I gingerly cradle the drum in my arms. "I promise I'll take good care of her."

"Just promise me you'll *use* her," he says, then adds with a grin, "What's the saying? Drum like no one's listening?"

"I will." I grin back, not pointing out the expression is slightly paraphrased.

The entire drive home, I feel like I'm soaring in the clouds. Wes was right about music being cathartic. A weight has been lifted that I hadn't realized I'd been carrying. I'm almost positive I don't even touch the ground when I step out of the town car.

"I'm pleased the lesson went so well." Javier places a hand on my elbow, probably to keep me from floating away.

"Thank you so much for arranging it. I had the best time." It's clearly an understatement, but I don't think there are any words in my vocabulary to adequately describe the afternoon.

"I look forward to getting together again." He bends down, and I brace myself for a goodbye kiss on both cheeks.

But instead, before I realize what's happening, he

briefly presses his lips to mine. I blink in bewilderment, completely caught off guard.

With a quick flash of his dizzying smile, Javier disappears into the town car, leaving me alone on the curb, too dazed to move.

From the corner of my eye, I catch a figure moving toward me. I blink again as my vision comes into focus.

The man walking his dog is Ethan.

And from the shocked look on his face, he witnessed everything.

11

The short trek through the lobby and subsequent ride in the elevator may have been the most awkward five minutes of my life. Other than a quick greeting, Ethan hasn't spoken a word. Not even to ask why I'm carrying a conga drum.

Part of me wonders if it's weird for him to see someone kiss me, like it would be weird to see some random guy kiss Brynn. Except, deep down, I suspect there's an entirely different reason. Only I'm not brave enough to dwell on what that reason might be.

Thankfully, the uncomfortable silence is broken by Brynn when we enter the apartment. "Yay! You're back! Where have you been?" She untangles her legs from sitting cross-legged on the floor cuddling Whiskers, and bundles the kitten into her arms to join me in the kitchen. Her eyes double in size when I set the conga drum on the counter. "Where'd you get that?"

"From Wes, the musician we saw at the lounge last night."

"No way!" she squeals. "Javier arranged a lesson?"

"He did. And Brynn, it was amazing." The rush of euphoria comes flooding back, and I can't help a giddy smile. "Easily one of the best days of my life."

Ethan makes a sound that's halfway between a snort and a harrumph as he unhooks Wilson's leash.

"What?" Brynn casts him an inquisitive glance. "What'd I miss?" Whiskers wiggles in her arms, and she sets her down to scamper off and play with Wilson.

"Nothing," I say hastily, shooting Ethan a silencing look.

But he has his back toward me as he hangs the leash on the hook by the door.

"Okay, now I *need* to know." Brynn leans forward, both forearms propped on the counter, her curious gaze darting between us. "Spill it."

"It's not a big deal," I insist, although heat creeps up my neck. "I think Ethan's insinuating that there's another reason I had the best day. But for the record, he couldn't be more wrong," I add with emphasis. Maybe a little more than strictly necessary.

"And what's the other reason?" Brynn asks. My blush must have deepened a darker shade of pink because she suddenly bolts upright and gasps. "It's about Javier, isn't it? Did something happen between you two?"

"Not exactly. He, uh, may have kinda sorta kissed

me when he dropped me off just now." I can't say the words without cringing a little.

Brynn shrieks and bounces on her toes in excitement as if I'd announced our engagement.

"Easy there." I hold up both hands and give her the universal "calm down" signal. "Don't get too excited. The kiss was completely unexpected and, honestly, unwelcome. Although I'm grateful he arranged a lesson with Wes, I don't plan on seeing him again."

"Why not? What's wrong with this one?" The way she says *this one*—in a labored breath—is thick with implications.

I can feel Ethan's eyes on me, and for some reason, the conversation is making me flustered and defensive. "Nothing is wrong with him. But I don't have to date every guy who crosses my path or does me a favor."

"No," Brynn retorts. "But maybe you could try dating *one* of them. Ever since Chad, it's like you've sworn off relationships. I'm starting to think you want to be single forever." Her tone is soft, threaded with concern, and I know she only wants the best for me, but her words still sting, and I can't help the tiny prick of indignation rising in my chest.

"And what's wrong with that? Being single isn't some disease that desperately needs a cure. Some of us are happier on our own."

Based on her dubious expression, she doesn't believe a word I said, and I can tell she's biting her tongue to avoid arguing further.

Ethan makes a big show of banging pots and pans behind us, loudly broadcasting that he's about to start dinner. When Brynn and I would argue as kids, he'd often step in with some silly distraction, and we'd eventually forget all about our quarrel. Not for the first time, I long for those simpler days, before the afflictions of adulthood calcified the once-soft edges around my heart.

"Speaking of being happy, I have some good news," Brynn offers, bridging the emotional divide.

"Let's hear it." I smile, grateful to put the disagreement behind us. I never could stay upset with her. Not even when she insisted my Barbie couldn't afford her dream house on a babysitter's salary and needed to downsize or sell her hot-pink convertible.

"Oliver felt bad when I told him I'd postponed our art class to help him at the office. So, to repay the favor, he offered to take us to the coolest art class in the city next weekend." Her eyes sparkle with a hint of mischief.

"I'm intrigued...." I trail off, waiting for her to elaborate.

Instead, she quips, "Great! But you'll have to live with the suspense. The only thing I'll say about it is to dress warm because we'll be outside."

I groan, not a fan of surprises. Although, I am grateful for the distraction. Trying to guess her mysterious outing will keep me from dwelling on the confusing mixed signals between me and Ethan—signals I'm too afraid to decipher.

The following week, I pepper her with questions, but she staunchly guards her secret. By the time we're standing in the Congo Forest Exhibit with Oliver and his zookeeper sister, Amy, I still have no clue what's going on.

But I have learned a few important things: one, Oliver and Amy Kim are half Korean born-and-bred New Yorkers, and two, Oliver and Brynn are hopelessly, undeniably head over heels in love with each other. They just don't know it yet.

The entire time Amy gives us a behind-the-scenes tour, Oliver sticks close to Brynn. He rarely takes his eyes off her for a second, and each time she smiles, his face lights up with delight. He hardly seems to notice the incredible, otherworldly setting around us.

Stepping into the immersive exhibit—inhaling the earthy scent of the verdant foliage, bracing against the cool mist of the waterfall, and even absorbing the strange, unfamiliar sounds—feels like we left the metal metropolis behind and have ventured into the wild, unfettered African jungle.

Amy guides us to a private cordoned-off area where three easels, each equipped with blank canvases and paint supplies, are waiting for us. But what stops me in my tracks is on the other side of the plexiglass viewing window separating us from the habitat. A massive gorilla, striking and grandiose in stature, gazes at us with dark, beady eyes that are at once warm and watchful, as if he's not quite sure what to make of us yet. I notice that he, too, has a blank canvas and easel, which I find baffling, to say the least.

"This is Kopi," Amy says proudly. "He's one of twenty western lowland gorillas here at the zoo. I know zookeepers aren't supposed to have favorites, but we all secretly do. Kopi is one of mine. And Andi, our giant anteater."

"Will we be painting Kopi?" I cast a nervous glance at the imposing primate. This won't come as a shock, but I've never been artistically gifted. I doubt I could manage to skillfully capture a convincing still life, let alone a live animal.

"Actually," Amy says with the eager energy of someone who loves their job, "Kopi isn't your subject matter. He's your instructor."

I stare blankly, positive I've misheard. Casting a quick glance at Brynn and Oliver, I wait for one of them to clarify, but they're both grinning broadly, as if they're privy to some inside joke.

"He's what?" I ask, not hiding my confusion.

"Your instructor," Amy repeats with a lighthearted laugh, delighting in my surprise. "All of our gorillas love to paint as part of their enrichment. They've each learned how to paint several different items, and are rewarded for participating. To them, it's a fun game. But Kopi is somewhat of a prodigy in the ape community. He's quite fastidious and takes his work very seriously. In fact, his pieces are so spectacular, they're regularly auctioned off to raise money for the zoo. And once a year, our top donors are treated to an art class similar to the one you'll be experiencing today."

"Isn't it amazing?" Brynn gushes, her brown eyes glimmering as she gazes at Oliver with open appreciation. "I couldn't believe it when Oliver explained it to me. Basically, Kopi is going to paint something and we follow along."

"Like a bigger, hairier Bob Ross," Oliver adds with a chuckle.

The eighties pop culture reference elicits a laugh from Brynn that's a little too loud considering I doubt she's ever heard of him. I only recognize the name because my parents made me watch his television show *The Joy of Painting* in an attempt to improve my embarrassing lack of artistic ability. Spoiler alert: it didn't work. But I mentally check off another box on the Proof Brynn Is Madly in Love list—laughing too hard at Oliver's jokes.

"Exactly." Amy nods her approval at their joint explanation. "And I suggest you follow along very closely. Kopi can be quite the perfectionist."

My body tenses as we each settle on one of the stools, getting acquainted with our supplies while another zookeeper—a lanky, bearded man named Travis—hands supplies to Kopi through a small opening Amy calls a "pass through," noting that we'll be using nontoxic paint.

How much of a perfectionist could a gorilla be? They aren't exactly known as the most graceful creatures in the animal kingdom. As he clumsily grips the paint-brush Travis hands him, I breathe a bit easier. With Kopi as our instructor, I'm going to guess the bar is set pretty low. So maybe I won't make a huge fool out of myself after all.

However, as Travis holds up an image of a bowl filled with glossy red apples, and Kopi dips his bristles into the crimson pigment with a slow, deliberate motion, I have second thoughts. Amy was right—his brushwork is downright masterful. While their opposable thumbs are common knowledge, who knew gorillas had so much dexterity? Or at least, *this* gorilla.

While I'm admiring his impressive detail work, a demoralizing thought hits me: I'm about to be bested by an ape.

Flashbacks to my many childhood failures invade my mind, and my fingers freeze above the canvas, completely immobile.

My parents were never the type to pin our artwork on the fridge. Instead, we had one place of honor on the mantel to display a single masterpiece at a time. Mom and Dad would judge our efforts on a variety of criteria from technique to composition, and the winner would be showcased for the entire month.

Let's just say, my work has yet to be featured.

The constant losses used to bother me, but after a while, I made my peace with it. Matt and Veronica won, fair and square. But losing to a primate who

unabashedly scratches his backside with his paint-
brush? How would I live it down?

I take a deep breath. I'm dangerously close to ditching
the class, which wouldn't be fair to Brynn, Oliver, or Amy,
who's been incredibly generous with her time.

Get a grip, Quincy. You can do this.

Latching on to a loose parallel, I take comfort in the
fact that we're in the Congo Forest section of the zoo,
drawing the coincidental connection to yesterday's
conga drum lesson. Recalling Wes's words of wisdom, I
remind myself to breathe and relax. *Breathe and relax.*

I repeat the mantra in my mind, and my stiff fingers
slowly limber as I mimic Kopi's movements. This is just
like drumming with Wes, I tell myself. Art is personal,
not perfection. Don't overthink it. Just *feel* it. Let the
brushstrokes find you.

I close my eyes and allow the bristles of the paint-
brush to do their thing, expecting my newfound, laid-
back mindset to transfer to the canvas the same way it
manifested in the studio with the conga drum. Except,
when we're finished and I take a peek at my handiwork,
I realize this is nothing like yesterday's experience. And
maybe painting with my eyes closed wasn't the best
idea I've ever had.

"If you're finished, please show your canvas to
Kopi," Amy tells us as we collectively set down our
brushes.

"We have to show him?" I gulp, not prepared to

have my work critiqued by anyone, let alone the wooly wunderkind, who, quite frankly, looks a little judgy for someone who relieves himself in public.

"Don't worry." She smiles kindly. "He's been trained to clap when he's shown someone's canvas. It's all part of the fun."

Sure. Fun. This is supposed to be fun, I silently remind myself.

I breathe a little easier when Brynn and Oliver take turns showing Kopi their work and he applauds in approval before lumbering toward Travis for a treat. Okay, this isn't so bad. He's actually kind of cute when he claps. And a hundred percent less intimidating.

Feeling more at ease, I rotate my canvas.

His prominent brow ridge lowers when he studies the chaotic splash of colors. Not a good sign. Apprehension punctuates each pulse of my heartbeat, creeping closer to panic mode until he raises his palms, poised to slap them together. I release a pent-up breath, my shoulders relaxing. But my relief is woefully short-lived.

Without warning, Kopi grabs a fistful of red paint and flings it against the glass while making a haunting, tormented sound. All of us, except Amy, jump backward in fright.

I've always known I'd never be the next Monet or Matisse. But I didn't know that one day my lack of artistic aptitude would send one of the most well-trained primates in the world into a full-blown meltdown.

12

"I'm so sorry," Amy says after directing us to turn our attention away from Kopi so we don't encourage his behavior, "Nothing like that has ever happened before."

"Please don't apologize. This is my fault." Humiliation scorches my skin, making me sweat beneath my thick coat. "I feel terrible that I upset him. I hope he's okay." Flushed, I loosen my scarf. I have a lot of experience dealing with embarrassing moments, but this one is proving more difficult to shake off.

"He'll be fine." Amy offers a gracious smile. "Just like us, they can occasionally have outbursts, and it's important that we remain calm and don't reward them with a reaction or they might learn to repeat the behavior. I'll quickly check to see if Travis needs help redirecting Kopi, then I'll walk you guys out."

She politely excuses herself for a moment, and I

stare at a crack in the ground, wishing I could slink inside and disappear. After yesterday's high point with Wes, this feels like a record-breaking low, and I'm not sure how to recover from the fall gracefully.

Oliver, sweet guy that he is, steps in and says with slightly exaggerated cheeriness, "Can I treat you ladies to dinner? There's a great Italian place not too far from here."

"Thank you, but we can't." Despite her best efforts, Brynn fails to mask her disappointment. "We're meeting a friend for a cooking class after this."

"Another time, then." Oliver maintains his chipper tone, although I sense he's equally crestfallen.

Clearly, these two want to spend more time together, and after today, I owe it to Brynn to make dinner with Oliver happen. "You go," I tell her. "Harper and I can take the cooking class."

"Oh, I couldn't—"

I have a feeling she's about to say something along the lines of "I couldn't abandon you in your time of need," albeit a bit more tactfully, but I interrupt before she has the chance. "I insist. You two go and have fun. I wouldn't mind spending some one-on-one time with Harper, anyway. Your two besties can bond over our favorite Brynn moments."

"Well…" Brynn chews her bottom lip, mulling it over, but I can tell she's softening to the idea. "I suppose it would be nice for you two to get to know each other better. That is, if you're sure you don't mind—"

"Go. Have a good time." Somehow, I manage to force a brightness into my voice that Brynn, thankfully, finds convincing. "Harper and I will have a great time together," I add for good measure.

The words of assurance are meant for Brynn's benefit, but when I check into the French cooking class in a trendy area of Brooklyn a short time later, I start to believe them myself.

The highly rated culinary school is located in an industrial-looking brick building that could've been a warehouse or factory in a previous life. But once inside, I'm dazzled by the sleek, bright, stylishly modern interior. Each cook station is equipped with individual ovens and gas ranges, and the ingredients neatly assembled on the pristine quartz countertops look like they're fresh from a farmers market.

Eager students are already milling about, chatting over the sort of soft, instrumental music you might hear in a Parisian café. An older couple fawns over our instructor, Chef Julia Blanchet, begging her to sign their cookbooks.

Although she's a New York native, the prestigious chef studied in Lyon, the gastronomical capital of France, and I was thrilled when Harper used her PR connections to snag us three spots in her class. Brynn must really like Oliver to miss out on this opportunity. Even I'm a tiny bit excited, although I can barely boil an egg. I remind myself I don't have to bake the best salmon with béarnaise sauce in the class. My one goal:

don't traumatize Chef Blanchet with my shoddy culinary skills and send her into a Kopi-esque conniption.

Oh, and don't burn the place down.

My phone buzzes in my back pocket, and I suspect it's Harper telling me she'll be a few minutes late. Which honestly doesn't surprise me. The woman is nothing if not fashionable.

When I read her text, my heartbeat falters.

> I'm so sorry. I hate to bail at the last minute, but I'm finally having dinner with Ethan! Please don't mention it to Brynn. I'll tell her at brunch tomorrow. You two have fun. And wish me luck!

She ends her text with a winking emoji, and never has a coquettish cartoon been more soul-crushing. I at once feel winded and overwrought, which leaves me breathless and a little light-headed.

Harper is having dinner with Ethan? And I'm stuck here. Alone. Could this day get any worse?

"Quincy?"

My blood freezes at the sound of a familiar voice.

Oh, please no. No, no, no....

Every fiber in my being revolts as I slowly turn around. "Hey, Sebastian."

"What are you doing here?" He doesn't hide his surprise.

"Learning to cook, I hope," I say with a wry smile, though my heart is crumbling. The culmination of the day's events have left me too distraught to deal with cat dander's number one nemesis.

My gaze drifts to the pretty blonde by his side. She's observing me warily, a possessive hand on his arm.

Sebastian tugs on his collar and clears his throat. "Quincy, this is Phoebe. We, uh, met on Spin," he says, almost guiltily. "In fact, this is our first date."

"How lovely." I shove all my angst deep inside, intent on surviving the cruel curveball life's lobbed my way. "A French cooking class is a great first date," I say, silently adding, *As long as you're not deathly allergic to butter.*

"Phoebe, this is Quincy." His tone holds a cryptic quality, and he curls his fingers, quite obviously miming a cat's claw.

Nice. Really subtle, Sebastian.

Phoebe's eyes widen in understanding. Clearly, he's told her all about me.

"Nice to meet you, Quincy." Her smile is equal parts pitying and patronizing. "Are you here alone?"

"Unfortunately, my friends had something come up at the last minute."

"Of course." She gives an exaggerated nod as if she isn't buying my transparent excuse. "That's too bad. But lucky for you, we're here." Gripping Sebastian's arm like a vise, she flashes me the same saccharine smile.

Yeah, lucky me. I force a smile in return, hoping it doesn't look as fake as it feels, then turn toward the front of the room as Chef Blanchet asks for our attention.

For most of the class, I focus on the task at hand, ignoring Sebastian's and Phoebe's flirtatious laughter and obligatory first-date small talk. I even mostly ignore the burning insecurity in the pit of my stomach trying to convince me that at this very moment, Ethan is falling hopelessly in love with Harper. But my newfound fortitude is exhausting, and it takes every ounce of self-control not to flee the waking nightmare.

The one saving grace? My béarnaise sauce doesn't look half-bad. Granted, it's lukewarm now, since it's taken me too long to properly prepare the lemon and parsley garnish, but when the timer chimes, I'm almost eager to slide the baking dish out of the oven and—my heart stops.

Instead of a beautifully baked salmon, I'm staring at pink, translucent flesh. Realization slaps me like a fish fin to the face.

I forgot to preheat the oven!

All my pent-up emotion—the humiliation and heartache—coalesces in that single second. Tears sting the backs of my eyes, but I can't lose control. Not here. Not now.

Sniffling, I swivel back toward the counter to grab the béarnaise sauce, hoping I can dump it over the raw fillet and none will be the wiser. But as I swiftly spin back around, I collide with Sebastian's elbow, and inadvertently douse myself with the thick, buttery sauce, splattering the front of my apron, the sleeve of my— sadly, dry-clean only—sweater, and my new suede boots.

I'm so mortified, I can't move.

And, of course, it's at that precise moment that Chef Blanchet pauses at our station to sample our work. She takes one look at my sticky sauce stain and says with the faintest accent from her time in France, "Everyone is born to eat, but not everyone is born to cook." Then, with a dismissive glance, she picks up a fork and digs the tines into the perfectly flaky flesh of Sebastian's salmon.

My chest squeezes, and adding insult to injury, Phoebe leans in and whispers, "On the bright side, you can take the raw fish home to feed all your cats."

13

I stare out the window in the back of the cab. Raindrops beat rhythmically against the glass, blurring the city lights beyond. Secluded in the shadows, I let silent tears trail down my cheeks while the driver yells at a sports announcer on the radio. I don't pay attention to which game is on or which landmarks we're passing by, oblivious to anything other than the abysmal failure that is my life.

Every harsh thought and nagging self-criticism crashes over me, pressing down on my chest, making it difficult to breathe. I feel like I'm drowning. Drowning in doubt. In disappointment. In the downfall of my grand delusions.

Why did I think I could do this? Moving to New York, the list, trying to evolve into a new me, a *better* me. It was all a mistake. A monumental, misguided, foolish mistake.

Maybe it's time to stop pretending and embrace the inevitable. Maybe it's time for Quincy the Quitter to do what she does best.

I exit the cab and stand frozen on the curb, letting the rain erase any trace of tears before I head inside, even though it's too early for Brynn or Ethan to be back from dinner.

In the dimly lit hallway, I turn the key in the lock, and my heart twists. Over the last several weeks, entering this apartment has felt like coming home. And now, it might be for the last time.

I ease open the front door, surprised to hear music on the other side. Frank Sinatra warbles his iconic love song to the city, "New York, New York," in an oh-so-ironic homage to my potentially final entrance.

In a moment of profound melancholy, I'm rooted to the floor, mentally noting the marked difference from the first time I laid eyes on Brynn's apartment, shrouded in shadows and unfamiliarity. Now, every inch radiates warmth and hominess.

Raindrops dapple the large picture windows and amber firelight illuminates Wilson and Whiskers, snoozing side by side on the soft shag rug in the living room. My throat tightens. I didn't think about leaving Wilson. And what about Whiskers? If I bring her back to LA with me, the inseparable pair will be an entire continent apart. Tears sting afresh as I consider everything—and everyone—I'd be leaving behind.

I quickly dry my eyes on my sleeve as I follow the

scent of sautéing garlic and onion to the kitchen and find Ethan chopping bell peppers at the center island. The scene is at once comforting and confounding. What is he doing home so early?

He smiles when he sees me, and my heart physically aches at the sight. Somehow, I'd managed to endure my entire adult life without his smile being the first thing I saw in the morning and the last thing I glimpsed when we bid each other goodnight. But as I look at him now, studying the slanted arch of his lips, the playful spark in his eyes, I don't know how I survived so long without it.

"Whoa." He regards my damp, bedraggled hair and the béarnaise sauce stain on my sweater. "What happened to you?"

"Cooking class casualty." I slide past him and shove the raw salmon in the fridge. "I got an A for effort and an F for edible."

"That's probably because you had the wrong teacher. I'll show you how to make a frittata that'll knock your socks off."

"Famous last words," I tease, but he isn't deterred.

"Before we get started, you need to change into proper cooking attire." He gestures to his plaid pajama bottoms and snug *Star Trek* T-shirt.

I crack a smile. "Your chef's whites look an awful lot like faded PJs."

"I like to run a comfortable kitchen, but don't let it fool you. The food is still five-star."

"Even if your sous chef has zero culinary skills?"

"We'll see about that."

Something in his easy smile makes me consider his offer. Although I've already checked off the cooking class, and technically never have to step foot in a kitchen again, if I so choose, I find myself changing out of my damp clothes and into the same flannel pajamas from my first night in the city, the ones with cartoonish mugs of hot chocolate and winking marshmallows.

When I rejoin Ethan in the kitchen, Frankie Boy is crooning "Let Me Try Again," as if he's taken it upon himself to sing the soundtrack of my life. I stand beside Ethan at the large center island, and he hands me a brown speckled egg.

"We need six whole eggs." He taps the side of a large ceramic mixing bowl.

"And by whole, you mean the egg whites, yolk, and the shell, right?"

"Although they're a good source of calcium, try to limit the amount of shell."

"I'll do my best." Not feeling optimistic, I whack the egg against the narrow rim, and the thick, translucent goo and plump yellow center plop into the bowl, along with a smattering of shell. *Figures.* With a sigh, I reach in and gingerly pluck them out, one sticky fragment at a time.

"Here. Let me show you a trick." Ethan places another egg in my palm. This one is a pretty muted-green color. "Instead of using the rim, give it one solid tap on the counter."

I shoot him a skeptical glance, but he nudges my arm. "Trust me."

Bracing myself for a slimy mess, I do as he says, but nothing appears to happen. I cock my wrist, preparing to try again, but Ethan places his hand over mine. A quick, sharp current zips up my arm, and I almost drop the egg.

"Hang on a sec." He turns my palm over, still cradling my hand in his. "See the tiny cracks?"

Sure enough, there's a web of sinewy fissures I hadn't noticed before. I nod mutely, too distracted by his touch to speak.

"Hold the egg over the bowl and gently press your thumbs on either side to break the membrane," he instructs. "Then slowly pull apart."

Although I hear every word he's saying, my limbs no longer function, as if the electrical current fried my mainframe.

"Here. It's not as tricky as it sounds." He positions himself behind me, so close the heat from his body radiates between us. It takes every ounce of my self-control not to lean back against him and soak it in.

With his hands over mine, he guides me through the motions, and the egg glides into the bowl without a single speck of shell to be seen.

"See. That wasn't so bad, was it?" Ethan steps away, and I immediately miss the warm, steady assurance of his presence.

He delegates the remainder of the eggs to me and

starts chopping basil. The sweet, potent scent permeates the kitchen, and I suddenly realize I'm starving. When was the last time I ate? My thoughts drift from my own missed meals to why Ethan is here, fixing dinner when he should be out with Harper.

"I thought you were having dinner with Harper tonight," I say casually, cracking the last egg into the bowl.

Ethan hands me a whisk. "That was her suggestion, but I prefer to meet in a coffee shop since it's easier to set up my laptop."

"Your laptop?" I pause midwhisk. Why would he bring his laptop on a date?

"Yeah." He shoots me a curious glance. "How else am I supposed to show her my sample websites? Sure, they're all mobile optimized, but you get a much better picture on a computer screen."

"Ethan," I say slowly, still bewildered. "Why would you show Harper websites you've designed? I mean, I understand you're proud of them, but isn't that a bit gauche for a first date?"

"It wasn't a date. She wants me to build a website for one of her clients. What made you think it was a date?"

I stare into the bowl of frothy, overly whisked eggs, thinking back to Harper's text. She sure made it *sound* like a date. Or had I completely misread it? Not wanting to bring her text into the conversation, I say, "Well, it's not so crazy to assume it was a date, is it? I mean, Harper is pretty perfect, don't you think?"

He shrugs. "I guess it depends on your definition of perfection."

"It's a fairly universally understood concept, Ethan. Obviously, I don't mean she's entirely devoid of faults. But she's beautiful, talented, accomplished, successful." For some reason, I'm ticking off her selling points like I'm trying to convince him to ask her out, and I can't figure out why. It's as if all my innermost insecurities have manifested in praise of another woman, a woman who's the epitome of everything I've always wanted to be but couldn't be more opposite. "Did you know she speaks five languages?" I blather on, unable to stop myself. "And she's competed in a triathlon. Twice. I bet she already knows how to crack an egg, too. I doubt there's anything she can't do, which basically makes her prime girlfriend material."

"I guess." Ethan layers the fresh herbs, bell peppers, and feta cheese evenly on the bottom of the cast iron skillet, then pours the egg mixture on top. "If you value those things."

I watch him work, his movements so nonchalant, so casual. There's something about the way he so easily dismisses all the characteristics and achievements I hold in high regard that rubs me the wrong way, as if everything I'd been taught to revere in life is worthless. "And you don't?" I ask, my tone challenging.

He slides the skillet into the oven, then turns to

meet my gaze, his expression measured and thoughtful. "Honestly? It doesn't matter to me if someone is good at everything. Are they kind? Compassionate? Do they love others well?" Using a dish towel, he sweeps the scattered shells into a pile to discard. "Perfection is a myth. We all have cracks, scars, and weaknesses. Just like we all have different strengths. But when you're a team, when you can lean on one another and help each other grow, that's when you've found someone special, someone worthy of forever."

His words wash over me, at once cleansing and utterly confusing, so contrary to everything I've ever known. In my world, worthiness was earned with accomplishments, by being the best. Ethan's sentiment, on the other hand, was simple and sincere, tempting, and, if I'm honest, almost too good to be true.

Silence settles between us, weighty and unwieldy, but I don't know what to say. My thoughts are too jumbled, too precarious.

It feels like I'm standing on the edge of a precipice. I could jump, but I have no idea what's beneath me, and more than a small part of me is afraid to find out.

14

After dinner, we carry our steaming mugs of hot chocolate to the living room. Rain taps against the windows, providing a soothing serenade. For a moment, I stand and admire my surroundings, digging my toes into the plush weave of the carpet. There's something magical, almost mesmerizing, about the way the city lights diffuse through the water droplets snaking down the glass.

Ethan scoots the large ottoman against the couch, creating a cozy corner to stretch out with his book. While there's plenty of room for two, I select a spot on the other side. My mind keeps mulling over our earlier conversation, and his words are starting to reshape my thoughts, like tumbling a sharp stone inside a rock polisher. What if he's right? What if I should focus less on striving for perfection and more on continual growth and, dare I say, finding enjoyment in the process? It's at least something to consider, isn't it?

Our presence stirs Wilson from sleep, and he leaps onto the couch to join us, wriggling onto the cushion beside me until he's nearly taking up the entire thing and I'm shoved a breath away from Ethan. Not to be left out, Whiskers scampers up the side, turns in a circle three times, then snuggles into Wilson's soft fur, purring contentedly.

I crack open the worn copy of *The Lion, the Witch and the Wardrobe* I borrowed from one of the bookshelves, and Ethan smiles.

"What?" I ask.

"Nothing. Just that this is what I remember most from when we were kids. You always had a book with you, like you preferred reading to spending time in the real world."

I color slightly at how well he knows me. "I suppose, in some ways, I did. When you read, you can be anyone you want. Someone funny or clever, adventurous and brave. Someone far more interesting than I ever was."

Ethan observes me over the rim of his mug, his gaze tender, but far too penetrating, as if he can see through me. I squirm and take a sip of hot chocolate, letting the sweet, syrupy liquid coat the back of my throat before asking, "What about you? If I remember correctly, you were quite the bookworm yourself."

"That's true. And in my own way, I enjoyed living vicariously through the characters, too. Mostly because they helped me see life through someone else's eyes. I guess you could say books helped teach me empathy."

I glance at the cover of the book he's holding. *Coffee, Crafts, and Creating Community*. I recognize it from perusing bestsellers in LAX before my flight to New York. It's a memoir by a woman who founded a coffee company in Costa Rica that focuses on giving back to the local community. Specifically, on how a simple craft project utilizing the empty burlap coffee sacks completely changed the trajectory of the company—and her life. It's exactly the sort of book I'd expect Ethan to read. And one of the many reasons I admire him.

"I want to show you something," I blurt impulsively, springing from the couch. I grab my laptop off the coffee table, and in my absence, Wilson stretches out a few more inches, commandeering my spot.

Ethan shifts his weight, making a smidge more room, and I settle beside him, trying not to be distracted by how incredible he smells. I flip open my laptop, suddenly nervous. "It's not completely finished yet, but I wanted to show you what I have so far." My heartbeat races as I pull up the campaign for MAD Market and hit Play on the video I'd been working on.

Carly Cannon, a pretty pop singer and B-list movie star, appears on screen. "I'm mad," she says into the camera over a moving instrumental soundtrack. "Mad about inhumane working conditions."

Her image fades, and José Chaves, a Triple-A baseball player recently recruited to the major leagues, materializes in her place. "I'm mad. Mad about exploitative business practices."

One by one, celebrities appear on screen vocalizing their concerns about worldwide issues that pertain to consumerism. In the final frame, they band together, Carly at the forefront. "And what are we going to do about it?" she asks, gazing directly at the viewer. "We're making a difference... one purchase at a time. Because where you spend your money matters."

The video closes with Ethan's MAD Market website, featuring the various business partnerships interspersed with snapshots of the social and environmental causes they support around the world. The final clip is a shot of his logo, and the words *Make A Difference* underneath, highlighting the meaningful acronym.

As the music fades, I steal a glance at Ethan, my heartbeat thrumming. At first, his expression is unreadable, an indecipherable mask of shock and disbelief. My breath catches in my throat. What if he didn't like it? What if he—

He reaches for my hand, and my thoughts vanish. For a moment, he merely holds it, squeezing gently, and when he finally speaks, his voice is raspy. "Q, this is incredible. I— How?"

I smile at his disjointed thoughts, a tingle of delight rippling through me. "I asked Brynn if she had any famous clients who might want to be involved. She reached out to them for me, and unsurprisingly, several of them loved the idea."

"I—I don't know what to say." His voice crackles, and he clears his throat. "I can't believe you did all this."

"I was happy to. What you're creating is special, Ethan. And I'm thrilled to be a small part of it."

He entwines our fingers, pressing our palms together tightly, and I can sense his gratitude in his touch. A warmth burns in my chest, spreading outward, radiating through my entire body.

For all the years I've worked for my family's advertising firm, I've designed ad campaigns with one purpose in mind: to impress my father and make him proud. But the look in Ethan's eyes as he replays the video evokes a feeling I've never experienced before, like my work has a greater purpose beyond garnering approval. Like I have the ability to do something that actually matters. And perhaps, poetically, that I can make a difference.

When the video ends for a second time, Ethan turns to meet my gaze. "You have a real gift for this, Q. And if it works out, and I can secure a meeting before you leave, I'd love to have you present this video to potential investors."

"I'd be honored."

He shakes his head as if he's still in awe, and says, "If your dad doesn't give you the promotion, he'll be making a huge mistake."

I bask in the glow of his compliment, marveling at how much can change in the span of a few hours. Earlier that evening, I'd contemplated leaving New

York, leaving my new life behind. And now, there's nothing I want more in this world than to stay right here, with Ethan. But whether I leave tonight or in a few weeks, like planned, this life is temporary. It was always temporary.

A reality I find far more devastating than I care to admit.

15

When I wake the next morning, something feels different. For starters, I've never slept so soundly in all my life. I'm snug and cozy, cocooned in a velvety throw blanket. Wilson snores softly by my side and— My heart stutters as my fingertips traverse a hard surface. A hard, softly rising surface.

I ease my eyes open, peeking beneath my lashes, barely daring to believe my own twenty-twenty vision. I'm curled against the warm contours of Ethan Delaney, my arm draped across his chest. His breathing is slow and steady, his lips slightly curled at the edges, hinting at a smile. There's a book askew on his lap, and I realize we must have fallen asleep last night while reading.

I hold my breath, not sure what to do. The logical part of my brain is saying I should move. I should quickly remove myself from the far-too-intimate position. I definitely shouldn't remain cuddled against him, savoring every small, scintillating sensation, pretending we live in a reality where we could fall asleep in each other's arms every night. But my heart? My heart threatens bodily harm if I so much as move a millimeter.

For better or worse, the decision is made for me.

The loud clang of a cupboard slamming shut startles Ethan awake. He bolts upright, dazed and unaware that he's inadvertently shoved me aside. His eyes are wide and unfocused, his hair adorably disheveled as he tries to discern his surroundings.

Meanwhile, Brynn continues to clamor in the kitchen, making coffee with twice the necessary volume. I'm going to guess all the ruckus has something to do with me and Ethan, and my heart sinks. On a surface level, I knew she didn't love the idea of Ethan dating one of her friends. But if I'm honest, deep down, buried somewhere beside my most naive hopes and dreams, I thought I might be an exception.

Clearly, I was wrong.

"Jeez, Brynn," Ethan groans, stretching his arms overhead. I try not to notice the way his T-shirt rides up, revealing a flash of his toned abs. "Are you making coffee or remodeling the kitchen? You're making enough noise for a construction crew."

She glowers and switches on the burr grinder. The cacophony of cracking coffee beans fills the air, stirring Wilson and Whiskers awake.

With the glorious moment of waking up in each

other's arms thoroughly relegated to the past, we throw on our coats and boots and take the "kids" outside to use the bathroom. As we cross the courtyard, my soles squish into the soggy earth. The cold air stings my cheeks but smells pleasantly sweet after the rain.

Ethan doesn't say much as we huddle side by side in the dog run, waiting for Wilson and Whiskers, and neither do I. But even in our silence, there seems to be this unspoken connection, a shift in the energy between us. I wish I could read his mind, to know where I stand, where *we* stand. But what would be the point? I'll be leaving soon. Besides, even if we wanted to explore the fragile, nebulous ledge extending beyond friendship, Brynn would never give her blessing. Which means the only recourse following our accidental slumber party is to pretend like it never happened—a strategy Brynn seems to support wholeheartedly.

On the cab ride to brunch, I wonder if she's going to confront or question the unusual sleeping arrangement she stumbled upon this morning, but she doesn't mention it once. In fact, she seems determined to converse about any topic other than me and Ethan. A predilection I'm happy to oblige, and when we meet Harper at the restaurant, I casually steer the conversation in another direction. "How was your date with Oliver?" I ask Brynn once we're settled at our table and finished with our preliminary chitchat.

She blushes and pretends to be engrossed by her bingo board, which isn't fooling anyone. Although

Brunch Bingo is now a weekly tradition, we never pay attention to the actual game.

"Date?" Harper immediately perks up, her board abandoned. "What date?"

"It wasn't a date," Brynn insists. "He invited Quincy, too, but she had to meet you for the cooking class."

Harper and I exchange a quick glance, and neither one of us seems eager to disclose the fact that she ditched me to meet with Ethan.

Before Brynn can quiz us about the class, Harper asks, "Well, why don't you ask Oliver out, then?"

"And humiliate myself when he turns me down?" Brynn sounds horrified by the suggestion. "No, thanks. Besides," she says, slowly sipping her pomegranate lemonade, "I've run a risk analysis, and it's not worth ruining a friendship over a relationship that will never last."

Maybe I'm reading into things, but her statement feels aimed in my direction. I choke down a bite of white chocolate and cranberry crepe, barely noticing the flavor.

Harper glances between us, sensing the tension, but has the good sense not to mention it. However, she should have mentioned *something*, because the lull in conversation leads Brynn to ask, "How was the cooking class?"

Now it's Harper's turn to squirm. "I, uh, didn't go."

"You didn't?" Brynn asks in surprise. "How come?"

"Something came up." She shifts in her seat,

fidgeting with the asymmetrical neckline of her effortlessly chic sweater. I've never seen Harper embody
anything other than perfect poise and confidence, and
frankly, her obvious discomfort is making me nervous.
It occurs to me that Brynn's reaction to Harper's confes-
sion may give me insight into my own predicament.

"I had coffee with Ethan," she admits, a little
guiltily.

"What?" Brynn sets down her knife and fork, her
food forgotten.

"It was strictly a business meeting," Harper assures
her. "I'd like him to design a website for one of my
clients."

This news relaxes the stiffness in Brynn's shoulders,
and she resumes cutting the Belgian waffle topped with
raspberry compote into bite-size pieces.

"But if I'm honest," Harper adds with a sigh, "I was
hoping it would turn into something more. Unfortunately, Ethan doesn't seem interested. My intuition tells
me he likes someone else."

Brynn's knife clatters against her plate, startling not
only me and Harper, but the couple at the nearby table.
After a pause, she picks it back up and stabs the poor,
unsuspecting waffle, slicing through the pillowy crust
with a ferocity that makes me feel sorry for it.

"Brynn, are you okay?" Harper asks meekly, clearly
feeling responsible for the sudden upset. Then, as if she
guessed the main source of Brynn's agitation, she adds,
"Do you know who Ethan likes?"

"Why don't you ask Quincy," Brynn mutters.

A sudden hot flash hits me as Harper glances in my direction, both eyebrows raised. I gulp my ice water, wishing I could elicit a distraction and make my escape. Hoping I sound more nonchalant than I feel, I say as calmly as possible, "I can explain what happened. It's not what you think." I gather a breath. "First, some background information. Sebastian, my disaster of a Spin date, was in the cooking class last night. On a date that was clearly going better than ours. I was so flustered, I forgot to turn on the oven, and let's just say, although I completed the class, it was an epic failure. When I got home, Ethan tried to cheer me up by teaching me how to make a frittata. Afterward, we talked and read in the living room and accidentally fell asleep. It was perfectly innocent."

"It didn't look innocent," Brynn mumbles.

"I know. And I'm sorry. But I promise, nothing happened. We're just friends." Which is the truth, I remind myself. Just because my emotions are muddled beyond belief doesn't change the facts.

Brynn sits quietly a moment, then softens. "Okay." She sounds like she *wants* to believe me more than she actually does, but before she can say anything else, her phone buzzes. She digs it out of her purse, checks the caller ID, then scoots back her chair. "Can one of you place the chips on my board for me? I have to take this."

"Sure," Harper offers, although I'm not sure it

matters. We're so far behind, we don't stand a chance at winning.

I breathe a sigh of relief when Brynn ambles toward the privacy of the hallway leading to the restrooms. Crisis averted.

Then I notice Harper studying me intently.

"What?" I dab the napkin to my chin in case I dribbled syrup.

"You should tell her," she says gently.

"Tell her what?"

"Look, Quincy. I like you. And even though this comes as a personal blow, I can put my own feelings aside for the greater good. Your friendship means a lot to Brynn. Since you arrived, she seems happier, more relaxed, and one degree less of a workaholic. I'd hate to see you two have a falling out because you're too afraid to tell her the truth."

"The truth?"

She holds my gaze, her countenance soft, almost empathetic, as she says, "You need to tell Brynn you're in love with her brother."

At the same moment, someone at a nearby table yells "Bingo!" as if punctuating her point.

I open my mouth to protest, but to my surprise and consternation, no words come out.

Could Harper be right? Am I in love with Ethan Delaney?

16

For the rest of brunch, I can't get Harper's words out of my head. They even haunt me on the cab ride to Bloomingdale's with Brynn afterward, an undercurrent pulling me deeper into my conflicted thoughts.

Since I cleared the air with Brynn about this morning, she's slipped back into her bright, chipper self, chatting nonstop about the upscale department store's big sales event. Apparently, she's mapped out an entire plan of attack, detailing the most efficient route through the store, complete with bathroom breaks.

By the time we've gone from designer shoes to evening wear, I'd changed my mind half a dozen times. While I tried on a pair of sparkly Jimmy Choo slingbacks, I realized I was definitely hopelessly in love with Ethan. And probably always had been, deep down. But an hour later, when I'd slipped into a sapphire-blue

Armani cocktail dress—that looked incredible, but I couldn't afford—I'd decided I'd merely confused my affection for Ethan with infatuation, which masqueraded as love but wasn't in actuality all that serious. When we finally reached outerwear, I didn't know what to believe anymore.

To make matters worse, all my indecision about Ethan had led to distracted shopping, which led to some serious overspending. The only bright side? Brynn assumed my addled state of mind stemmed from sales-tag oversaturation, and I simply couldn't decide which items to buy.

"What do you think of this?" I turn sideways, observing every angle in the full-length mirror. The weighty wool jacket engulfs my entire frame, from the fluffy, faux fur–lined collar to the ankle-grazing hemline.

Brynn frowns. "It's nice, but winter is almost over. Sure, you like the coat now, but you'll quit wearing it soon."

In the reflection, I watch her study the detailed floral embroidery on the Alice and Olivia coat she's wearing. Is it just me, or is there subtext behind her words?

"Besides," she adds, as if it's an afterthought, "you won't need a heavy winter jacket like that when you're back in LA."

The statement, though true, stings a little, and I'm not sure why it evokes such a visceral reaction.

Suddenly sweltering, I shrug out of the thousand-pound straitjacket. "You're right." I stab the coat hanger back into the sleeves and shove it onto the rack with the other discards. Turning back to Brynn, I say, "You should get it. It looks really good on you."

"I don't know..." Her voice fades in her hesitation. "It's kind of a statement piece. I don't think I can pull off something so flashy." She wriggles out of the coat. Between the shimmery satin and all-over applique, it's certainly a showstopper. But too flashy? While it's not her style per se, the Brynn I knew would wear whatever she wanted with confidence.

"You can totally pull it off," I assure her, but she's already returning it to the rack.

Growing up, Brynn was never arrogant or boastful, although she certainly could have been considering she crushed every math competition, got straight As in every subject, and surpassed all the other kids in our gymnastics class, executing a perfect backflip while I struggled with cartwheels. Not to mention she once made a grown man cry with her stirring violin solo of "Ave Maria." Okay, so the man was our sentimental, soft-hearted music teacher who openly wept when we watched *The Sound of Music* on the last day of school, but still. Brynn is one of the most talented and lovely human beings on the planet. It doesn't make sense that she'd be insecure about anything, let alone a fancy coat. What had shaken her confidence?

"I think I'm ready for a brief shopping intermission," she says, changing the subject and, surprisingly, veering from her master plan. "Let's grab a cupcake at Magnolia Bakery."

Although we had brunch not too long ago, I follow her to the escalator. As we head down to the main floor, our arms draped with Bloomingdale's iconic brown paper bags, a thought occurs to me. Maybe I've taken our easy, uncomplicated friendship for granted. Sure, we seemed to fall in sync the second we reconnected, but we've been out of touch for a long time. A lot can change in a few years.

Once we reach Magnolia Bakery, and revel in the mouthwatering aromas as we wait in line, Brynn selects a red velvet cupcake and I opt for their famous banana pudding. It takes some expert shuffling of our shopping bags, but we decide to walk off some calories while we eat by perusing the beauty department.

Determined to get to know adult Brynn better, I lead with the first topic that comes to mind. "How are your parents? I haven't seen them since..." I pause, searching my memory. "Since you last came home for Christmas, what was it? Three or four years ago?"

She picks up a sample bottle of perfume, sniffs, then makes a face, setting it back on the counter. "They're okay, I guess."

Hmm... So, she's not feeling particularly talkative about her parents. But I try one more time, anyway. "Do they still go on those murder mystery–themed train tours in Napa?" Mr. and Mrs. Delaney were fanatical about murder mysteries. They even hosted annual costume parties where someone "died" over dinner and the guests had to solve the crime. My parents were invited once, but even though Brynn and I were best friends, our parents never really bonded, which, considering their vastly different life philosophies, never surprised me.

"No, they don't," she says, spritzing Chanel N°5 on her wrist. The complex fragrance, both floral and musky, blends with the sweet scent of my banana pudding. It's an intoxicating combination, but Brynn doesn't seem to notice. Her features are strained as she adds, "They actually, uh, got divorced. Almost two years ago."

The news hits me with such shocking force, I nearly drop a hundred-dollar bottle of perfume. "What?" I stare dumbly, unable to wrap my head around the revelation. The Delaneys were the perfect family. I always thought her parents would wind up like the old couple in *The Notebook*. Hopefully without Alzheimer's, but so lovingly devoted, they leave this world together, embraced in one another's arms.

"Ethan and I were shocked, too," Brynn admits.

"What happened?" I ask gently, almost in a whisper.

She shrugs. "Nothing, really. They said they just... drifted apart." For the first time since the conversation started, she turns to look at me, her brown eyes muddied with pain. "It's crazy, you know. How two people can promise to spend their lives together, then give up like that. They didn't even try counseling. They just threw everything away because... I don't even know why. Because they didn't have the same hobbies anymore?"

She sounds so confused, so dejected, my heart aches for her. "I'm so sorry, Brynn. Is that why you haven't come home in a while?"

"Ethan and I didn't want to split the holidays between their two places, so we decided to make them come to us."

"I can't believe I had no idea." My tone is apologetic, thick with remorse. Why hadn't she told me? Or rather, why hadn't I asked?

She shrugs again. "We're both busy. It never came up."

What she means is, we lost touch and stopped sharing all the important moments in our lives. We'd drifted apart. Just like her parents.

I suddenly have a flashback to fourth grade summer camp. We'd made matching tie-dyed T-shirts and friendship bracelets out of green and purple thread and tiny pink beads, accessories to signify our lifelong bond. Whatever happened to those?

"I should've made time for you, for our friendship." As I say the words, there's a warmth in my chest, a fiery conviction that burns so much stronger than a youthful sentiment. I've experienced life without her, felt the loss, and I don't want to make that mistake again. "I'm so incredibly sorry I lost touch."

"Me, too." Her voice is low, laden with sincerity.

"Never again?" I shift my bags to one arm and hold out my free hand.

"Deal." She does the same, and we slap palms, snap twice, then wiggle our fingertips together, exactly how we used to seal important agreements when we were kids. Feeling a little silly as we revert to our childhood in front of the perfume counter at Bloomingdale's, we share a sheepish laugh.

"Ready to go?" Brynn asks, tossing her paper cupcake wrapper in the recycling bin.

"Not yet." I follow suit with my cardboard pudding container and grab her hand. "There's something we need to do first." I tug her back toward the escalator.

"What's that?"

"We're getting you that flashy coat because the Brynn Delaney I know can not only pull it off but looks amazing in it."

She grins, revealing the slight gap between her two front teeth, and in that moment, she's the same Brynn from our youth. The Brynn who still believed in happy endings and the permanence of a person's promise.

I've let her down before, more than once.

And I make a silent pledge to never let it happen again.

17

The next morning, I skip my run with Ethan under the guise of needing to work on my ad campaign. And it's not a total ruse. Although my main reason is to give my heart some much-needed time and distance to figure things out, I do need to focus on Extra Energy Drink. I still haven't thought of a slogan, let alone designed an entire campaign. I've tried to focus on their all-natural ingredients and the gentler, plant-based energy-boosting compounds, but I can't think of anything that doesn't feel prosaic and over-done. Which means even if I check off every single item on my list, it's a moot point if I don't have a pitch for the competition.

I tuck myself away in my room, only surfacing for an occasional snack and bathroom break. When daylight slips into the dim of evening, I slink into the kitchen, weary and dry-eyed from staring at my laptop screen for too long.

"You okay?" Ethan asks when he takes one look at my harried appearance.

I can only imagine the state of my hair since I'd combed my fingers through it in frustration all afternoon. And I vaguely recall losing a few popcorn kernels in my clothing as I mindlessly munched on endless handfuls. I brush the crumbs from my baggy sweater and sweatpants, which is definitely not the most flattering outfit I own. "I've been better. I've been racking my brain all day for the perfect catchphrase, but my mind is blank."

Ethan adds plump shrimp to a pan of melted butter and garlic. They spurt and sizzle, sending the most tantalizing aroma into the air. "Try not to stress about it. And give yourself a break. The right words will come at the right time. Often when you least expect them."

"Next you're probably going to tell me to use the Force," I tease, climbing onto the barstool to watch his culinary skills in action.

"Funny, you are," he says in his best Yoda impression. "But I was actually going to tell you what you really need is a good meal."

"I won't argue with that." I grin, grateful for nourishment other than junk food.

He grabs a pair of tongs and places a mound of angel hair pasta on a plate, followed by a generous serving of

the buttery shrimp. After adding a pinch of fresh parsley, he slides the plate toward me and hands me a fork.

Leaning forward, I inhale the fragrant steam, my
mouth watering. "I don't think I can ever go back to
cooking for myself," I say without thinking.

"You know you don't have to," he says quietly.

I whip my head back, meeting his gaze. His eyes
search mine, asking an unspoken question. A foolish,
reckless part of me wants him to ask me to stay. But
why? What would be the point?

A muscle flexes along his jawline, the precursor to
his next thought.

I inch toward him on the barstool, practically
hanging off the end.

But before he can speak, the front door flies open.

"I have a problem," Brynn announces as she barges
inside, a ball of agitated energy.

Our connection broken, Ethan moves back to the
stove and fixes another plate of pasta.

Burying my disappointment at her penchant for bad
timing, I turn my attention to Brynn. "What's wrong?"

"Oliver invited me to the St. Valentine Skate-a-thon
this Friday night." She attempts to unravel her scarf
from around her neck, but is so frazzled, she only winds
it tighter. Her arms flail in frustration as she struggles to
extricate herself from a face full of flannel and fringe.

While I have no idea what a skate-a-thon is, that's
not my most pressing question. "Oliver invited you out
on Valentine's Day?"

"Yes. No. Maybe. I don't know." She finally frees herself, releasing a heavy exhale of relief as she hangs her scarf on the hook.

"What do you mean you don't know?"

"I think it might be a date, but I didn't know that at first." Shamefaced, she shrugs out of her coat.

"What did you do?" I say in my best scolding schoolteacher voice.

"I invited you to come with us."

"What?" This is worse than I thought.

"I know, I know. The words sort of just... came out." She flops onto the barstool beside me. "He ran into me at the coffee cart and said his sister told him about this fundraiser for the zoo at The Rink at Rockefeller Center and asked if I'd be interested in going. So, I said, 'Sure. Sounds fun. Quincy and I would love to go.'"

I cringe, and she slumps forward on the counter, face-planting onto her forearms. "And that's not the worst of it," she groans.

Gathering a breath, I brace myself. "And what's the worst part?"

"The Skate-a-thon is a couples event," she explains, albeit a bit muffled as she's still facedown, her mouth pressed against her sleeve. "You're supposed to skate in pairs, holding hands the entire time. If you let go or stop skating, you're disqualified. The last couple on the ice wins."

"Sounds romantic," I blurt offhand, then realize my mistake.

Brynn whimpers, and it strikes me that she actually *wants* to go on this date. Which, considering her previous reservations with all things Oliver related, is a huge step for her. "There's an easy solution," I say calmly. "I'll stay home so you and Oliver can skate together."

"Yeah, that would've been a good idea." She slowly lifts her head, and her sheepish expression tells me I'm not going to like whatever she says next. "But I didn't think of that at the time, so I came up with a different solution."

"Which is...?"

"I said you'd be bringing a date." This time, she has the decency to look contrite.

"Oh, Brynn. You didn't," I moan.

"I'm sorry. I realize now I should've made an excuse for why you couldn't go after all, but by the time I thought of that, he'd already bought two extra tickets online. Maybe you can ask Javier?"

"No way," I say hastily, then add after a moment's thought, "But maybe Harper will go with me."

"I'll go," Ethan says casually.

Brynn and I swivel toward him in surprise, as if we'd both forgotten he was there. He leans against the back counter, twirling the spindly noodles with his fork tines, his lips quirked in amusement.

"Um..." Brynn darts her gaze between us, a spark of panic in her eyes. "I don't think that's a good idea."

"Why not? You need someone else to go with you, and I happen to be free."

"But it's not really your thing," Brynn insists, trying a little too hard to sway him against the idea. "I doubt you'll enjoy it."

"Oh, I don't know about that." He grins, and to my horror, glances in my direction.

Heat sweeps across my cheeks, and even though I divert my attention to the tangled web of pasta on my plate, I can feel Brynn's gaze bore into me.

Part of me feels like I should jump in and say something to fix the situation.... But what, exactly?

"Then it's settled," Ethan says when Brynn runs out of reasons to protest. "You can be Oliver's date, and I'll be Quincy's."

Although his tone is lighthearted and teasing, the way he phrases his summation makes my cheeks flame even hotter, and I pray he doesn't notice. Or Brynn, for that matter.

"And tell Oliver I'll pay him back for our tickets," he adds. "What kind of date would I be if I let another guy pay for us?"

I make the mistake of glancing up at that precise moment and catch Ethan's playful wink.

He's clearly hamming up the whole date angle like it's some kind of hilarious joke, but there's something hidden in his eyes—a furtive flicker—that makes me suspect a deeper motive than he's letting on.

And despite my best intentions to keep things between us strictly platonic, the possibility makes me shiver.

18

Although I've seen The Rink at Rockefeller Center in movies, nothing compares to being on the ice, basking in the glow of lights as they glitter across the frozen surface. For a moment, I simply stand there, clutching the railing, in complete awe of my surroundings. The recessed rink appears to sink even lower into the earth as lustrous skyscrapers loom against an inky black sky, accentuating the breathtaking contrast of darkness and light.

But what's even more unexpected is the towering Christmas tree, magnificent and magical in its size and splendor.

"I'm surprised to see the Christmas tree in February," I tell Ethan, though I'm certainly not sorry to see it. The shimmering bulbs reflect a mesmerizing array of pinks, purples, and reds, perfectly aligned with the Valentine's Day theme.

"It's not usually still up this time of year, but an endangered bird built a nest in the branches, and an animal rights group convinced the city to leave it up until the eggs hatch, rather than risk harming them by trying to relocate it."

"Well, I'm glad. I've always wanted to see it in person."

"It's pretty impressive. Even more so at Christmas. But then, all of New York is impressive at Christmastime."

"I'm sure," I murmur, secretly imagining what it would be like to spend the holidays together. We'd bundle up for the stunning light show in the Botanical Garden, catch *A Christmas Carol* on Broadway, and marvel at the elaborate window displays at stores like Barneys and Saks Fifth Avenue while we shop for the perfect gift.

"Okay, enough stalling," Ethan says, holding out his hand. "The competition is about to start."

"Maybe we should just forfeit now." I glance over my shoulder at Brynn and Oliver. They both look adorably nervous, and as I watch Brynn fiddle with her gloves, I feel both proud and apprehensive. Is this a small taste of what a parent experiences when their child is about to embark on their first date?

"Why would we do that?" Ethan asks, drawing my attention back to our conversation.

"Because I don't know how to skate. And it's probably too risky to traverse a slippery surface with a novice who has sharp blades strapped to her feet."

"Without risk, there's no reward." His eyes are twinkling, and there's something in his tone that makes me shiver, but he's moved on before I can dwell on any hidden meaning. "Besides, I can teach you."

I consider his proposition, vaguely recalling his brief stint on a junior hockey team when we were younger. "I guess we can give it a try."

"Gee, thanks for your vote of confidence in my teaching skills," he teases, offering his hand again. He isn't wearing gloves, and for a moment, I regret donning mine.

I weave my fingers through his, and the pressure of his palm against mine sends a strange flutter through my stomach. *Focus, Quincy.* As I glance over my shoulder again, I catch Brynn watching us, her brow knit with worry. The butterflies in my stomach twist themselves into an uncomfortable knot.

"Ready?" Ethan asks as a loud trumpet blare announces the start of the skate-a-thon.

I tear my gaze from Brynn and give a shaky nod. "Ready," I lie, not only ill prepared to skate, but seemingly unable to suppress my growing feelings for Ethan, no matter how taboo and disastrous.

He pushes off the ice, towing me along as "Can't Help Falling in Love" by the King pours out of the speakers.

My legs are wobbly at first, but as we glide around

the rink, my nerves wane, and I take comfort in the belief that Ethan's abundance of skill can make up for my complete lack thereof. But before we've made it halfway around, Ethan's skates fly out from under him and he slams onto his back, yanking me on top of him.

"Ow," he groans, rubbing the back of his head.

"What happened?" I gasp, grateful his solid frame broke my fall.

"Did I mention that I don't know how to skate, either?"

"What? But you said you'd teach me!"

"I figured I'd learn on the job."

"What about hockey?"

"That was years ago. And I wasn't any good then, either."

I gape at him, completely incredulous. Then, laughter bubbles in my chest, bursting out before I can stop it. Ethan joins me, his body shaking with laughter beneath me.

Couples skate by with looks of concern, and one pair seems like they're about to stop and help—which, considering their kindness would cost them the competition—is quite sacrificial. But when they realize we're not only fine, but in near hysterics, they speed past us.

"I can't believe you lied to me." I wipe a tear of laughter from my eye, still propped up on his chest.

"I didn't lie, per se. I was overly confident in my ability to ice-skate on the fly."

"You could've told me you didn't know how."

"But would you have still wanted me to be your partner?"

I'm suddenly at a loss for words. Is Ethan implying that he risked life and limb so he could be my skating partner? And if so, why? He could've done any number of things tonight, but he chose to be here with me and was now possibly paralyzed.

I'm about to do something really foolish and ask him, but I glimpse Brynn and Oliver skating toward us.

"Are you all right?" Brynn calls out.

Before they can stop to help, I say quickly, "We're fine. Keep skating or you'll be disqualified." Regretfully, I push myself off Ethan, and clumsily struggle to my feet.

He does the same, and we both look like newborn foals learning to stand for the first time, all bumbling limbs and zero sense of balance.

"Are you sure?" Oliver asks, slowing his gait without stopping.

"Positive." I hobble toward the rail, then fling myself against it like a drowning victim clutching a lifeline.

Ethan joins me, then waves them on. "You guys go. Brynn needs to restore some dignity to the Delaney name."

"I'll see what I can do," she teases as they swish across the ice, leaving us in their wake.

"What now?" I shuffle toward the exit, eager to escape the mob of skaters zipping past us.

"Get some hot chocolate and cheer them on?"

"Sounds perfect."

A few minutes later, we're cradling warm paper cups brimming with rich, creamy chocolate, watching Brynn and Oliver circle the rink. Brynn's cheeks are flushed from the cold, her eyes bright, and she hasn't stopped smiling in half an hour. I've never seen her look so happy.

"How come Brynn is such a great skater and you're..." I trail off, smiling as I recall our epic tumble.

"So good at falling?" His eyes are twinkling again, to an almost dizzying effect.

I direct my attention back to the ice. "Sure," I say, smiling behind the brim of my cup, "let's go with that."

"Brynn and Harper come here every year. I never made the time before."

My heartbeat does a funny little skip when he says *before*, and I can't help reading into it. Does he mean before *me*?

"And what about hockey?"

"It was short-lived. When my parents saw I wasn't enjoying it anymore, they pulled me from the team."

"I've always envied that about your parents. They never had any expectations. They simply wanted you to enjoy life."

He's quiet for a moment, as though he's mulling over my words. When he finally speaks, his voice is soft, almost sorrowful. "There's a downside to only sticking with something until the shine wears off."

Although he's speaking in generalities, I instantly read the subtext.

"I'm so sorry about your parents, Ethan." I lay a hand on his arm. "I couldn't believe it when Brynn told me."

"She took it pretty hard. Honestly, I worry about her sometimes. I know she gave you a hard time about Chad, but I think she was projecting her own feelings onto you. Ever since Mom and Dad split, it's like she doesn't believe in love anymore."

"I know the feeling," I murmur softly, momentarily lost in my own thoughts. It's uncanny how you can go from complete certainty in someone to losing all sense of control, every assurance slipping through your fingertips like a faint tendril of mist.

"What happened with him?" His tone is even and easygoing, but his gaze is intent, giving away the depth of his interest.

"Things didn't work out," I say simply, hoping I sound relaxed and unconcerned, like it's long forgotten, a thing of the past.

"Did you end it?"

I hesitate, briefly tempted to lie. But I don't want any dishonesty between us, with a rare exception for the occasional embellishment about one's ice-skating skills. "He did."

His hand clenches around the cup, creating an indent in the sides. "What possible reason could he have for breaking up with you?"

He sounds so indignant. I'd smile if the memory wasn't so painful. "I'd say he had about a million and one reasons." I swallow, flashing back to Chad's main reason—the reason that still haunts me because every word he said rang true. "But long story short," I continue, dragging myself back from the past, "I made a great girlfriend, but didn't have long-term potential."

"He said that?" Ethan's grip tenses again, this time dislodging the lid of his cup, sloshing hot chocolate onto his hand. He doesn't even flinch when the steaming liquid touches his skin.

I shrug, not sure what to say, and take a sip, hoping to soothe the tightness in my throat.

"I'm sorry, Q. The guy's a jerk." His tone is gravelly, a mix of anger on my behalf and a protective tenderness, and for some reason, his reaction numbs some of the pain.

"It's okay. We all have our stories of love gone wrong." I force a brightness into my voice, trying to lighten the mood. Yet, I can't silence my own curiosity. "What about you? Why aren't you married with six kids by now?"

"It's not because I don't believe in love, I'll tell you that," he says without hesitation. "When the timing's right, I want the whole package. Someone who'll be my teammate and best friend, kids who will hopefully take after their mother, a dog or two, if I can't steal Wilson from Brynn." He grins, and I'm transfixed by the sudden shift in his countenance. When he talks about the

NEW YORK, NEW YEAR, NEW YOU 157

future, there's a radiant, almost dogged hopefulness
that mystifies and entices me at the same time. What I
wouldn't give to experience even a fraction of his faith.

He looks down, stilling my breath with his smile.
"I'm glad you came to New York. You've been good for
Brynn. Before you came, she never would've gone out
with Oliver. And I hate to say it, but I kinda like the
guy."

"So do I."

He reaches for my free hand, holding it gently in his
as he laces our fingers together. "You're a good
friend, Q."

His compliment should make me happy, but
instead, my heart aches. I drop my gaze to our entwined
hands, fighting a slight sting in my eyes as Ilene Woods
purrs "So This Is Love" in her silky contralto.

A good friend. If that were true, I wouldn't be flirting
with fate, toying with the temptation of something
beyond friendship with Ethan. For both their sakes, I
need to stop this from going any further.

Summoning a smile, I say, "So are you," knowing
he'll understand exactly what I mean: *You're a good
friend and it's all you'll ever be.*

A sentiment that feels all the more painful when
contrasted with how close we came to something more.

19

By the following week, the status quo had returned to normal. At least, whatever normal used to be before our conversation on Valentine's Day, the moment I sensed Ethan was about to reveal his feelings for me ran deeper than friendship.

As I expected, he read between the lines of my comment and hasn't made any overtures since then. In fact, our interactions have been so benign and platonic —even when immersed in the intimacy of his bedroom while building my blog—I can't help wondering if I'd imagined the connection between us, and it's a thought that fills me with both relief and regret.

"How much longer?" I pant, barely able to lift my legs as I trail behind Ethan on our longest practice run yet—twelve torturous miles. While my stamina has improved since we started training, I don't think I'll ever be one of those gazelle-like runners who make marathons look easy.

"Not too much farther. And you'll like this last stretch." He tosses an encouraging grin over his shoulder.

To his credit, he's kept the terrain interesting each time we train, and I've seen almost every inch of Central Park. I once asked him why we haven't run the official route of the Big Manhattan Marathon since, according to my research, that's how most participants of the more popular New York City Marathon prefer to practice. Ethan said he finds it more enjoyable—and thus easier—if the course is fresh. And on the bright side, it means we haven't encountered the Gapstow Bridge again.

When we near the Mall, the long promenade leading to Bethesda Terrace, I forget all about my aching feet. Barren elm trees arch over the wide walkway. Their wet branches, still dappled with water droplets from last night's rain, sparkle in the early morning sunlight.

Although breathing is a struggle, I inhale the sweet, earthy scent, exhaling slowly. The sharp pain in my side subsides as I repeat the measured breaths, but my endurance is fading fast. "I don't know if I'm going to make it much farther," I confess, feeling discouraged for multiple reasons. I'd hoped the run would clear my head, allowing the perfect campaign slogan to spring to the surface. But I feel even more at a loss than before we started, and I'm starting to panic. I've even tried music therapy, thumping away on Wes's drum until my palms hurt. And yet, still no epiphany.

After all this time and effort completing the tasks on my list, I could still lose the competition. Which would mean I have no hope of crossing off the final item, the one I'd impulsively scribbled on Christmas Day.

"Then I think it's time for your last lesson," Ethan says with a dramatic flair. "See that statue up ahead?" He points to the bronze figure of William Shakespeare, and I nod.

"Make that your target. Don't think about how much farther you have to run, just make it to the statue."

"Okay. I'll try anything." I follow his lead, although I'm not sure I understand the method to his madness, and I reach the marker sooner than I thought. "That wasn't so bad," I admit, feeling slightly energized.

"Great. Now that's your new target." He gestures to the burnished form of another famous writer, which is only a short distance away.

I lock my gaze on the landmark and reach it with surprising ease. We repeat the exercise until we surpass the stretch of statues dubbed the Literary Walk, when Ethan switches to more unusual targets like a woman seated on a bench feeding the birds and a saxophone player filling the park with his mellifluous melodies.

"I can't believe your technique is working," I say when the beauty of Bethesda Terrace comes into view with all its stunning stonework and impressive fountain focal point.

"Oh, ye of little faith." Ethan chuckles. "It's simple psychology. Breaking a goal into smaller, more manageable steps makes it less daunting. So, next time you feel like giving up, tell yourself to take one more step. Then take one more."

We cross the imaginary finish line, and a rush of adrenaline surges through me as Ethan's words ignite an idea so inspired, I can't help cheering out loud.

"See. Feels great to finish, doesn't it?" he asks, mistaking the reason for my excitement. "You did great. And if you can handle today's run, you'll complete the marathon, no problem."

I grin back at him, so giddy over finally having a winning slogan, I can barely contain myself. "Thank you, thank you!" Without thinking, I plant a kiss on his cheek.

His eyes widen in surprise. "Uh, you're welcome."

Eager to get back and buckle down—and distract myself from how warm and enticing his skin felt against my lips—I turn on my heel and sprint in the direction we came. "Race you home!"

By the time I've showered and changed, the entire marketing campaign has materialized in my mind. And I have to say, it's pretty brilliant. The kind of brilliant that might actually garner me the promotion.

And I owe it all to Ethan.

With only a few finishing touches left, I close my

laptop and slip into the kitchen, inspired to cook Ethan dinner as a thank-you. After all, the man's love language is clearly food.

The apartment is still and quiet, the glow from the city shimmering through the tall picture windows. I flick on the kitchen light, adjusting to the brightness.

With Ethan out on a walk with Wilson and Whiskers, who perches inside his coat pocket, I only have twenty minutes or so to accomplish my task.

Brynn is working late again, and I'm not entirely sure if it's because she's actually busy or if she's avoiding me. Ever since her sort-of date with Oliver at the skate-a-thon on Friday, she's been distant, almost melancholy. But whenever I ask her about it, she evades the topic like a money launderer avoiding the IRS, a comparison I know she'd appreciate. My only hope is that with enough time and persistence, I'll find out what happened.

I pull up "New York State of Mind" on my phone, then grab an onion and bulb of garlic, trying to recall all the necessary ingredients. With any luck, by the time Ethan gets back, the apartment will be flooded with the mouthwatering aroma of a perfectly baked frittata and the smooth vocal styling of Billy Joel.

Except, when Ethan walks in with Wilson and Whiskers, he's met with the piercing screech of an alarm and the acrid scent of smoke.

"What happened?" He quickly unleashes Wilson

and sets Whiskers on the floor before rushing over. "You okay?"

A thick black cloud billows from the skillet on the stove, and no matter how frantically I flap the oven mitt, it only seems to grow stronger. "Just dandy," I say with sarcasm, still flailing my arms like I'm waving in a Boeing 737 for a safe landing.

Ethan deftly grabs a kitchen towel, using it as a makeshift oven mitt as he moves the skillet off the burner. Then, he flicks on the hood vent above the stove, and the smoke immediately starts to dissipate.

He surveys the chaos littering the countertops—shards of eggshell, loose onion skins, and a spilled jar of pepper kernels, among other things—waiting for the alarm to subside, signally the crisis is over.

When it emits its last shrill beep, he asks, "Is that a frittata?" as he eyes the smoldering skillet.

"In its former life." Except for one inexplicable spot in the center that's still raw and gooey, the rest is charred black. "It was supposed to be a gesture of appreciation, but it looks more like a death threat than a thank-you."

His features soften, and to my horror, he grabs a fork.

"What are you doing?" I shriek, hoping he's not about to do what I think he's about to do.

"Eating my thank-you frittata." The scorched exterior crunches as he digs in the tines, and I cringe.

"You're not really going to eat that, are you?"

"Of course I am. You made it for me." He brings the fork to his mouth, and I bury my face in my hands, too mortified to watch. "Mm..."

Peeking through my fingers, I can't help chuckling as he chews the clump of charcoal, trying not to choke on it. "Okay, you did your good deed for the day. You can put the fork down now."

"Why would I do that? It's delicious." He goes back for a second bite, this time stabbing the slimy part.

"Don't eat that!" I lunge toward him, trying to swat it out of his hand before he gets food poisoning.

We tussle over the utensil until he's backed me against the counter, his hand clasping my wrist. His face is mere inches from mine, our breath ragged.

In that moment, every thought, every well-rehearsed reason why we can't be together, escapes my mind and is replaced by a visceral need to lean in closer, to press my lips to his. The need is so intense, so all-consuming, fear suddenly grips me. Fear of my desire, of the unknown, of the consequences of surrendering to a reckless impulse.

Twisting my wrist out of his grasp, I duck beneath his arm, fleeing the situation along with my own muddled emotions.

"Pizza?" I grab my phone and search for a delivery option, grateful for the excuse to avoid his questioning gaze.

"Sure." It's remarkable how one syllable can convey so much disappointment and confusion.

My vision glazes over as I scroll through the search results, not registering a single word. I hear the smooth glide of a drawer opening, followed by a rustling sound, then Ethan hands me an old-fashioned paper menu. "Thanks." I still can't bring myself to look at him.

"Tell me which kind you want, and I'll place the order. The number's programmed in my phone."

"Do you still like thick crust?" I ask, dragging my finger down the list of toppings, struggling to concentrate. I can still feel his touch, the warmth of his breath, the white-hot glint in his eyes that made every inch of my skin blaze.

"When I'm visiting my folks back home. But in New York, I stick with the thin, crispy style crust. They say there's something in the city's water that gives it a special flavor. Minerals, I guess."

He's gallantly trying to lighten the mood, and the least I can do is help him out. I lift my gaze, attempting a breezy smile. Although, there's a good chance it looks slightly crazed, since I can't quite get my lips to cooperate. "I'll let you order, then. Whatever you usually get."

"Sounds good."

Twenty-five minutes later—after a joint effort to restore the desecrated kitchen to its former luster—Ethan lifts the cardboard lid of the pizza box, releasing a ribbon of aromatic steam. The sauce is light and silky, the cheese slightly golden, the spices fresh and fragrant. My stomach growls as he sets an enormous slice on my plate. "Okay, you have to admit this looks better than my burnt frittata," I say, poking fun at myself.

"What do you mean? That frittata was a work of art. Totally worth the chipped tooth."

He flashes his adorably slanted smile, and the world rights itself again. Maybe we can salvage the evening after all.

As if on cue, Brynn trudges through the front door, her expression weary as she removes her coat and scarf.

Ethan and I exchange a glance, and as if he can read my mind, he slides two slices of pizza onto a plate and slips away to his room, giving us time alone.

"Rough day?" I ask while Brynn pours herself a glass of water.

"It was okay."

I select a prime slice of pizza for her, then tap the barstool next to me. "Sit. Eat. Let's talk."

She sighs heavily but relents.

"What happened between you and Oliver?" I decide the direct approach is best.

"Nothing, really," she says with a shrug. "I just decided I wanted to stay friends." She folds her pizza in half and takes a bite. Her eyes close, and for a moment, some of the strain in her features melts away.

"We'll come back to that. But what happened that prompted that decision?" I press, remembering how, even as kids, she'd circle around a sensitive topic to avoid hitting the most tender spot.

"While we were skating, there was this perfect

moment," she says, after a reflective pause. "The crisp air, the sparkling lights, that really pretty Etta James song... 'At Last,' I think it's called. It was like her words were just for us. Anyway, it was the kind of moment that makes you hold your breath and wish it would never end."

"Okay," I say slowly, not following her train of thought. "And that's a bad thing?" There had to be more to the story.

She stares down at her pizza as if she's trying to memorize the exact number of basil leaves. "Oliver squeezed my hand and said, 'This is the kind of first date you tell your kids about.'"

"Oh." I try to match her crestfallen tone, but I'm more confused than ever. "I don't understand. That sounds sweet."

"It is. But don't you get it? He said kids, Quincy. *Kids*. He's the kind of guy who dates a girl to the altar."

"And I repeat, that's a bad thing?"

"It is when I don't think I ever want to get married."

Now I understand. "Oh, Brynn." I reach for her hand, my heart aching over her lost faith in love. "Not every marriage ends in divorce."

"Over forty-four percent of them do. And as someone who's obsessed with numbers, I don't like those odds."

I can tell she's hunkered down on her position, and I'm not going to change her mind in this one conversation. So, I put a pin in it for now.

"Tell me this, Miss Numbers," I say, lifting my slice of pizza. "If I fold this in half, will I be consuming half the calories?"

"Of course." She takes a bite of her own slice, smiling for the first time in days.

For the rest of the evening, we talk and laugh about anything and everything, until I'm positive thoughts of Oliver have faded into the background, and I realize how much I missed this—being present for the little moments. Little moments that count in a big way.

Sure, we can still talk on the phone when I'm in LA, but I doubt it'll be the same. And I'm starting to wonder...

Is the promotion—and the possibility of finally making my father proud—worth losing a friend who sees the real me, inside and out, and not only loves me unconditionally, but actually *likes* me, too?

Some days, I'm not so sure.

20

The next several weeks zip by in a blur, my private blog keeping record, preserving my memories in simple HTML code. Brynn and I squeeze in every last second of time together before I have to head back home. She even joins me for my dance class. I thought I'd signed up for Salsa Dancing for the Advanced but hadn't noticed the ellipsis when I'd registered online. Turns out, if I'd have clicked to read more of the description, I would've seen that we were actually attending Salsa Dancing for the Advanced *in Years*. Brynn and I were the only students under sixty-five, but we had a blast, anyway, even though all my dance moves were abysmal.

To keep from constantly collapsing in tears, we made a pact not to discuss my impending departure, which was easier said than done. One or both of us would often tear up at the most random moments, then pretend like we had an eyelash or piece of lint stuck in our eye. But we both knew what the tears were really about.

Like now, as I gaze at myself in the mirror, dressed in head-to-toe running gear, I feel my throat tighten.

Only three more days until I head back home.

Home...

The once simple word feels so complicated now, and the image conjured in my mind is an incongruent amalgamation of two different places. I wish I didn't have to choose between them.

I see Whiskers in the reflection, curled in a tiny ball on the bed, purring contentedly, oblivious to the fact that in a few short days she'll be leaving the only home she's ever known. While I'm hopeful she'll adjust to life in LA, my heart still breaks at the thought.

There's a knock at the door, and I quickly dry my eyes on my sleeve. "Come in."

Brynn pokes her head inside, leaning against the doorframe. One look at me, and her features crumple.

"Don't cry or I'm going to cry," I scold, my voice strained.

"I can't believe you're finally running the marathon. And I'm going to miss it." She sniffles, trying to hold herself together.

"With tax day in two weeks, it's hardly your fault. We'll celebrate tomorrow."

"That's right." She manages a small smile, but it

quickly falters as she murmurs, "Over our last Brunch Bingo before you—"

"Don't say it!"

"Okay, okay." She dabs her eyes with the lapel of her blazer. Then, she steps all the way into the room, revealing what she'd kept hidden behind the doorjamb. A glossy black garment bag.

"What's that?"

"A little something to say I'm proud of you." She tugs on the zipper. "I thought you could wear it to your celebratory dinner with Ethan tonight."

As she sweeps the garment bag aside like a ceremonial curtain, I suck in a breath. It's the stunning, sapphire-blue cocktail dress from Bloomingdale's—the one I'd drooled over but could never justify buying myself.

"Brynn, this is too much," I say, although I can't help caressing the silky soft fabric. "Besides, I doubt Ethan is taking me somewhere this fancy simply to celebrate me finishing the marathon."

Her gaze softens, and when she speaks, her voice is low, almost a whisper. "Not only that."

"What do you mean?"

Hesitation flickers in her eyes, like she's not sure how much she should reveal. "Let's just say, I know my brother. And wherever he takes you, this dress will be perfect." She holds my gaze a moment longer and adds softly, "I hope you two have a really good time."

My heartbeat skips, then stops altogether. Is she—

Did she...? I blink, wondering if I'm reading into things. It almost sounds like Brynn gave us her blessing. And I honestly don't know how I feel about the possibility. At a loss for words, I pull her into an embrace, the dress pressed between us, and murmur a simple but earnest thank-you.

"Break a leg today," she says, borrowing the common showbiz sentiment for good luck before thinking better of it. "Or, maybe *don't* break a leg."

"Thanks," I laugh. "I'll do my best."

"You're going to do great. I told Ethan to record you crossing the finish line."

"For proof?" I tease.

"No, you cynic. Because I hate that I'm missing it. I know you'll finish." She pauses before adding gently, "You're not the same person you used to be, Q. And I don't merely mean from when we were kids. You've grown even during these past few months. I don't think I've told you this, but I admire you tremendously. And seeing how brave you've been has given me a lot to think about. About myself and about how much I'm going to miss you."

Tears cascade down my cheeks now, but I don't care. I throw my arms around her again, and for a moment, we simply cry together, finally allowing ourselves to grieve our inevitable goodbye.

Her words release something inside of me—the tightly clenched fear that no matter how hard I try, I'll still be seen as Quincy the Quitter, the girl you can't count on.

Encouraged, I carry her words with me, metaphorically tucked in my pocket as I complete mile after mile. When my muscles ache and my feet throb, I pick a spot in the distance and press forward, remembering that regardless of the past, I'm capable of more than I once believed.

It isn't until the course rounds a corner that my resolve wavers. The mass of runners before me appear to rise toward the skyline as they ascend the Gapstow Bridge, cresting at the top, then disappearing down the other side.

I stop abruptly, causing another runner to bump into me. We both mumble an apology, and he runs on ahead. But I can't move.

My labored breath becomes even more ragged, and my chest squeezes painfully. I close my eyes. *It's only a bridge, Quincy.* A mechanism to get from one side of the pond to the other. It's not some formative fixture in your life that holds power over you.

I open my eyes, forcing myself to take in the sturdy stone arch. It looks so different in spring, beautiful, even, to a casual observer. Against the backdrop of vibrant greens and blossoming branches, it's easy to see why it's a popular proposal spot. To most people, it marks a new beginning, the start of something wonderful. To me, it signifies the end—the end of hope, of an unattainable future.

I think of Ethan waiting for me at the finish line. He believes I can do this.

I *can* do this.

Gathering a shaky breath, I move one foot forward, then another, until I break into a run. Each time my rubber soles pound against the stone, images flash in my mind, tiny shards of disjointed memories.

Chad's smile, so boyish and brash.

Thud. My heel hits the ground, carrying me closer to the bridge's summit.

Another vision flickers, sharp and quick like a knife.

Chad falls to one knee. There's a glimmer of something shiny and metallic.

Stop! Stop! Stop! I press both hands to my temples, willing the memories away. Burying them with thoughts of Ethan—a beacon of hope and subtle strength—I manage to make it down the other side. My pace quickens, leaving the bridge even further behind, further into the past where it belongs.

Suddenly, I experience a strange burst of energy. Gone is the fatigue, the heaviness, the strain. Harnessing what must be the legendary second wind, I sprint toward the finish line.

Ethan is waiting just beyond the billowing balloon archway, the most enticing sight I've ever seen.

But he isn't alone.

21

Ethan envelops me in a hug as soon as I cross the finish line, and I'm still so stunned, it takes me a moment to process what's happening.

"Congrats, Q! You did it!" He pulls back, his grin bursting with pride. "And I recorded the homestretch for Brynn, otherwise she'd kill me."

"I recorded it, too. For Mom and Dad." Matt stuffs his phone back in his pocket while I stare, completely dumbfounded. "They wanted to be here but send their congrats."

"Yeah, congratulations," Veronica says with a smidge less sincerity. "I honestly didn't think you'd finish."

I choose to overlook that comment, too thrilled to see them. "I can't believe you guys came all the way out here to watch my race." When I'd mentioned the marathon as part of my Christmas Commitments accountability, I had zero inkling they might show up.

"Of course we did. It's not every day your little sister runs a marathon." Matt beams at me, and there isn't a hint of irony or sarcasm in his voice. I expect him to follow up with something snarky, or a veiled insult, at least. But he doesn't.

To my embarrassment, my throat tightens. Tears simmer beneath the surface, but if I cry now, that will surely unleash the teasing. So, I do my best to tamp down my emotions. "Thanks. It means a lot to me that you're here."

"Well," Veronica quips, "Dad offered to pay for our tickets, so we'd be crazy to pass up a free trip to New York."

Ah, good ol' Veronica. Leave it to sister dearest to put a damper on a perfect moment. But even so, they're here. And I choose to focus on the positive.

"He's also paying for dinner," Matt adds. "I've already made reservations at the hottest restaurant in the city."

"Oh." I glance at Ethan, instantly torn. I don't want to interfere with his plans. I've been looking forward to them all day. But Matt has never done anything this nice before. And when you've waited your whole life for a gesture like this one, it's hard to turn it down.

Ethan seems to read my mind. "That sounds great, Matt. Quincy deserves it. You guys have fun."

His generous and selfless heart never ceases to

amaze me. "Matt," I say, linking my arm with Ethan's. "Can you add one more to your reservation? Ethan deserves a celebratory dinner as much as I do. Without his training, I never would've made it this far."

"No problem. I'll call right now." Matt digs out his phone again.

"Thanks, Q." Ethan squeezes my arm. "I have to make a call, too. Excuse me a sec." He steps a few feet out of earshot, and my heart sinks a little. He's probably calling to cancel our dinner plans. Once again, I feel like I'm faced with a choice between my old life back home and my new one in New York. My old, lifelong desires and my newly realized ones.

"All set," Matt says crisply. "Our reservation is at seven."

"Where are we going?" I ask.

"It's a surprise. But you're going to love it." Matt puffs out his chest a little when he tells me, "I had to pull some major strings to get us in."

I feel the telltale tears threatening to spoil the moment again. Despite extending several invitations over the years, I've never shared a meal with my siblings without our parents being present. And to think, tonight we're not only having dinner together, it's a celebratory dinner in my honor. I could pinch myself, but then I'd also have to kick myself for ruining a good thing. "Do you want to come see the apartment? You can meet Wilson and Whiskers." I hold my breath, hopeful the dream will continue. I'd love to share this part of my life with them.

Matt looks like he's about to accept, but Veronica cuts in. "We need to check into the hotel. We'll meet you at the restaurant, okay?"

"Okay." I smile, suppressing my disappointment with the reminder that it's a miracle they're even here at all. "See you then." We're not really a hugging family, but I lean in for one, anyway. Veronica stiffens, but it could be because I'm damp with sweat.

Matt, on the other hand, gives me a big bear hug, the kind that lifts my feet off the ground. "Congrats again, Quince. You looked great out there." His words wrap around me like a thick blanket, and even when he sets me back down, my arms linger a little before letting go.

On the walk home, I feel like I'm floating, buoyed by both my own personal achievement and the miraculous appearance of my siblings. I can't stop babbling about the race and bouncing on my toes in excitement. Ethan matches my enthusiasm, although he warns me that once the euphoria wears off, every inch of my body will be sore. To help curb the inflammation and replenish my nutrients, he advises a cool shower, and fixes me this odd concoction of oats, peanut butter, sliced banana, and some other ingredients I don't recognize, which turns out to be surprisingly delicious for something so healthy.

To Ethan, these probably feel like small, simple

gestures, nothing more than helping out a friend. But to me, they're everything. I've never felt more cared for than during the months I've spent here with Ethan. And in a family that's always trying to get ahead of the other person, to be the *best*, it's almost surreal to have someone put your needs above their own.

Like tonight, for example. Ethan didn't hesitate to set aside his own plans in favor of Matt's, knowing how much my brother's efforts mean to me. Even though there's a part of me that feels foolish to hope, I still can't extinguish the dream that one day, my siblings and I will have a relationship like his and Brynn's. And as we walk into the restaurant to meet them, I instinctively grab Ethan's hand. "Thank you."

"For what?"

"For this. For coming here. For *being* here." Suddenly, I have this overwhelming urge to pour out my heart, to say all the things I've thought over the past few months, but never had the courage to say out loud.

But the moment passes, and Ethan is holding open the door for me. "I'm honored to tag along." He grins, giving off a sort of casual, teasing vibe, like a joke between friends.

But as I brush past him into the restaurant, he leans in and whispers so close to my ear, I can feel his breath on my neck, "You look incredible, by the way." His voice is low, gravelly, and anything but casual.

I shiver, and goose bumps scatter across my bare arms, though I'm the furthest thing from cold.

"Hey, guys! Over here." Matt waves us toward the bar area. They're standing at a high-top table, four drinks waiting. "Our table is almost ready. But they have to give us the spiel first."

"Spiel?" I ask.

"Yeah, you know. Explain how it all works."

I glance at Ethan, but he looks equally baffled. This isn't our first time eating at a restaurant. It's not like they need to show us how to use a knife and fork.

"Is that Armani?" Veronica asks, eyeing my attire with a mixture of surprise and envy.

"It is." I smooth the silky bodice. "You like it?"

"It's nice," she says with a shrug, downplaying her initial reaction as she smooths the hemline of her basic black cocktail dress.

Between the two of us, she's always had the superior wardrobe, but for once, thanks to Brynn, I'm not the least-stylish sister. My skin tingles as I recall Ethan's whispered compliment from seconds earlier.

"Carmichael, party of four?" A tall, spindly man wearing dark sunglasses approaches our table.

"Yes, that's us." Matt raises his hand.

"Welcome to Media Nocte." The man accentuates the restaurant's name in a way that makes it sound Latin or Italian. "Is this your first time dining with us?"

"It is," Matt says, once again speaking for the group.

"Excellent. We always love virgin blood." The man grins, and I wonder, not for the first time, why he's wearing sunglasses inside. "I'm Rowen, and I'll be your server this evening. Tonight's menu is a five-course meal, preselected for your dining pleasure."

Wow. Five courses? Matt wasn't kidding when he said this place was fancy. Once again, I'm touched and impressed by the gesture.

"Media Nocte is Latin for *midnight*, and it's our great pleasure to be your first dining-in-the-dark experience."

Wait. Our what?

"By consuming your meal entirely in the dark," Rowen continues, "each flavor is enhanced and accentuated by your lack of sight."

My heart stops. Did he say we'd be eating dinner in the *dark*?

As if reading my mind, Rowen says, "I assure you, the experience is quite safe. So, if you hear someone scream, please don't be alarmed. One of your fellow patrons has merely stabbed themselves with a steak knife."

Matt and Veronica laugh at the server's dark-humored joke, but I haven't heard a word since he said we'd be dining in the dark. Without lights. Sans the ability to see. I can't think of any other ways to communicate my worst nightmare.

"In all seriousness," Rowen continues, "safety is our highest priority. Well, that and the finest, most inventive cuisine in New York. All our servers, including myself, are legally blind, which means we're quite skilled at navigating without sight. We guide you to your table and will help you locate your seats and silverware. There are also glow-in-the-dark markers that lead to the restrooms and emergency exits. However, please only use them if absolutely necessary, since it makes it harder for us to maneuver safely. Lastly, to maintain the integrity of your dining-in-the-dark experience, we ask that you surrender your cell phones in the lockers provided. They may be retrieved at the end of your meal." He gestures toward a wall of small metal cubbies with keypads. "I'll give you a moment to finish your drinks and dispose of your cell phones and will return shortly to escort you to your table."

"See. Told you this was the hottest restaurant in town." Matt beams. "How cool is dining in the dark?"

"You can't be serious." Ethan's voice is dripping with disapproval.

"What do you mean?" Matt asks innocently.

"This is so typical of you two," Ethan mutters. When it's obvious Matt didn't hear him, he says a little more loudly, "Quincy is afraid of the dark, Matt."

"Really? Since when?"

"Since forever." Ethan sounds really irritated now, and I don't bother mentioning that my fear of the dark only stems from the time I got locked in a closet for four hours during a game of hide-and-seek when I was five. A game where neither of my siblings ever intended to look for me.

"Shoot. I'm sorry, Quince. I forgot. I feel like a jerk." His remorse is so sincere, I make an on-the-spot, completely reckless decision.

"It's okay. Honestly, it's not as bad as it used to be. Let's stay." I remind myself that my fear of the dark is only paralyzing when it's pitch black, and I doubt the restaurant is *completely* devoid of light.

"Are you sure?" Ethan places a hand on my arm. "We can go somewhere else."

"Where are we going to get last-minute reservations on a Saturday night?" Veronica asks, but closes her mouth when Ethan shoots her a silencing glare.

"Ethan's right," Matt says. "Let's eat somewhere else."

I'm touched by his willingness, knowing it was tough for him to get this reservation. And if he cancels now, at the eleventh hour, he isn't likely to get them again, either. "Thanks. I appreciate that. But I'll be fine," I insist, trying to convince myself more than anyone when, in reality, this could quite easily be one of the worst decisions I've ever made.

22

Rowen leads us into the main dining area conga-line style. Except, instead of hands on waists, he has Matt place a hand on his shoulder, followed by Veronica, then me, and lastly, Ethan.

His hand feels hot against my bare skin, and I try not to melt beneath his touch as his fingertips graze my collarbone.

Once inside, I'm struck by the complete and utter darkness. If there's something blacker than pitch, this is it. Apart from the dots on the floor, glowing faintly, I can't see anything, not even a single silhouette. My throat goes dry.

"It's fine. Everything's fine," I whisper under my breath, reminding myself I'm not trapped, and I can leave whenever I want.

Ethan applies firm, steady pressure to my shoulder,

reassuring me of his presence, and I breathe a little easier.

Although the room is deprived of even the faintest glimmer of light, it isn't devoid of sound. The din of laughter, conversation, and the clinking of flatware against china hums around us, at once foreign and familiar. I never realized how much I took my sight for granted, and it's an unusual experience to suddenly find myself without it.

Rowen guides each of us to our seat, in turn placing our hand on the water glass, plate, and utensils, familiarizing us with the layout of the table.

"How often do people spill their water?" I ask Rowen with a nervous laugh.

"Not as often as you'd think."

While I take comfort in that knowledge, I also know if anyone *were* to spill their beverage tonight, I'd be the most likely culprit.

Once we're situated, Rowen leaves us with the promise he'll return shortly with our first course.

"I don't think I'm the right demographic for this experience." Veronica's voice lilts on my left. "What's the point of getting dressed up for dinner if no one can see you?"

"Because it's all about the food," Matt tells her. "Just wait until you taste it. All the reviews say it's unreal, like you suddenly have superhero taste buds."

"I'd read that comic book," Ethan laughs.

"What's the tagline?" I ask. "Faster than a speeding

bullet. More powerful than a locomotive. Able to taste every ingredient in a single bite."

Matt and Ethan laugh at my variation of Super-man's catchphrase, and the comforting sound eases some of my lingering apprehension. There's a small chance I might actually enjoy myself.

By the time the food arrives, I've *almost* forgotten I can't see my hand in front of my face, let alone my fork. Rowen helps me find it again, and after I stab around my plate for a few moments, I finally bring my first bite to my lips. Notes of citrus and cardamom burst across my tongue, followed by something I don't recognize. The intense flavors swirl in my mouth, both savory and sweet, in an intoxicating combination. I have no idea what I'm eating, but I do know one thing: I can't get enough of it.

After we've had fun trying to guess our first course, Matt surprises me by saying, "Let's all make a toast to Quincy."

"Another great idea, Matt," Ethan says jovially. Although similar in age, they weren't that close when we were growing up. My heart warms to see—or rather, *hear*—them getting along. It may be greedy to want my new life in New York *and* a relationship with my siblings, but I can't help holding on to the dream. And catching a glimpse, like tonight, only makes me cling tighter.

"Lead the way, Delaney," Matt tells him, equally affable.

"To Quincy," Ethan says, and I picture him raising his glass. "You've tackled a new city and new experiences, pushing yourself out of your comfort zone. While it hasn't always been easy, you haven't backed down. You've met each new challenge with courage, grace, and humor. And I couldn't admire you more."

"Hear! Hear!" Matt cheers, and for once, I'm thankful for the darkness so no one can see my tears of happiness. Hands down, this is one of the best nights of my life, and I never want it to end.

"To Quincy." Matt's deep voice carries across the table. "It's no secret you used to lack follow-through. And I admit, I didn't think we'd see you cross that finish line today."

For a moment, I flash back to all those Christmases we sat side by side in the living room, waiting to report on our Christmas Commitments. My stomach clenches with a similar foreboding, preparing for more of Matt's trademark teasing.

"But when you did," he continues, "I realized how far you've come. Literally over twenty-six miles." He chuckles, then adds with a more serious tone, "But it wasn't the physical distance that's most impressive. You've come far as a person. And I'm proud of you, Quince."

I dab my eyes with my napkin, though no one can see my tears. I don't think my brother has ever said anything so kind, let alone so complimentary, and I bask in his words, savoring the sweet sound of his approval. Over the past few months, I may have learned I don't *need* it, but I'd be lying to say it wasn't wonderful all the same.

To my left, Veronica clears her throat, and I hold my breath, wondering if the impossible is about to happen. To my recollection, my sister has never paid me a single compliment that wasn't backhanded, and I'm both eager and anxious to hear what she's about to say.

"I'm proud of you, too, Quincy," she says, sounding almost sincere. "A marathon is a huge accomplishment. Especially since I don't think I've ever seen you run. Unless you count the time you chased after that taco truck."

Matt and Veronica share a laugh, but I don't join them. While her anecdote is true, and I'd made a similar joke to Ethan several weeks ago, I don't find it humorous this time.

"Although..." She trails off thoughtfully. "There was the time we were camping at Lake Arrowhead and tricked you into thinking a bear was trying to tear through your tent. You took off running so fast, you didn't even bother putting your pants on."

"I forgot about that!" Matt rumbles with laughter.

My cheeks burn now and tears prick my eyes for an entirely different reason than before. The perfect evening—the one where we enjoyed each other's company as adults, as *equals*—has evaporated like a hazy memory.

"I think you're missing the point of a toast, Veronica." Ethan's voice is a low, angry growl.

"Sorry, I got sidetracked," she says, not sounding sorry at all. "To Quincy. For choosing to run for reasons other than fear or food."

"Hear! Hear!" Matt echoes, as if her words were all in good fun.

A moment of silence follows, and I realize they're waiting for me to say something, but a response eludes me. Ethan finds my hand and gives it a squeeze of solidarity. Drawing strength from his grasp, I swallow the tightness in my throat. "Thank you all for being here and for this fabulous meal." While I truly hope I sound sincere, I'm starting to lose any desire to salvage the evening. Right now, I just want to go home.

As if their unkind words were never spoken, my comment elicits another round of guesses as to what our next course will be, and I take the opportunity to excuse myself to use the restroom. I need a few minutes to splash water on my face and reset.

But as I follow the dim markers away from the safety of our table, farther into the sea of black, the darkness envelops me. I've only made it a few steps by the time my feet stop working, glued to the floor in panic. I'm about to turn back when I hear Ethan mutter angrily, "What's the matter with you two?"

"Excuse me?" Veronica huffs.

"You're supposed to be celebrating Quincy's accomplishment, yet all you've done is put her down."

"We're only joking around," Matt says, sounding a tad defensive.

"Yeah. Quincy knows it's all in good fun," Veronica adds, and I balk at the way she speaks for me. I certainly would not describe it as *fun*.

"Maybe she does. But a person can only take so much of your particular brand of humor. And I, for one, have had enough."

I know I shouldn't be eavesdropping, but I can't help myself and shuffle closer, forgetting all about my fear of the dark. And that I need to stick firmly to the guide markers on the floor.

There were a few times when we were younger where Ethan called out Matt and Veronica's bad behavior, and they didn't take it well then, either.

"Then it's a good thing you're not the boss, isn't it?"

I nearly laugh out loud at Veronica's juvenile comeback. I imagine her at ten years old, both arms crossed, her blue eyes narrowed and defiant as she shouts, "You're not the boss of me, Ethan Delaney!" before sticking out her tongue.

When Ethan speaks again, his voice is softer, almost weary. "Don't you think it's time to grow up and put all this jealousy behind you? All Quincy ever wanted was your respect and friendship. You're her big sister, Veronica. She looks up to you. And yet, thanks to you and your constant put-downs, she can't see how incredible she is."

My breath catches in my throat. Ethan thinks I'm

incredible? There's something in his tone when he says it—a tender conviction—that makes my knees tremble slightly. Instinctively, I take a step toward the sound of his voice, and at that exact moment, collide with a heavy object.

I hear a grunt, then the loud clang of something heavy and metallic hitting the floor, followed by shattering glass. A startled woman screams, and in the commotion and confusion, someone flicks on the lights.

I wince as my eyes adjust to the brightness, then cringe as accusatory stares dart in my direction.

"Are you okay?" Rowen asks.

"I'm fine. But I'm so, so sorry, Rowen. I got up to use the restroom and must've veered from the markers." Every inch of my body burns with embarrassment, both from ruining everyone's dining experience and because I was quite clearly caught eavesdropping.

"It's all right, ma'am. These things happen. Please return to your table and we'll clean this up."

Brimming with remorse, I cast a contrite glance at the mangled remnants of our second course while two women dressed in solid white emerge from the kitchen, and head straight for us.

"I'm so sorry," I mumble again, slinking back to my seat, although I can't imagine sitting through the rest of the meal with Matt and Veronica after everything that just transpired.

Apparently, Veronica had the same thought. "We

should go, Matt. I'm sure we've all lost our appetite."
She scrapes back her chair and stands.

"But it's prepaid," Matt protests.

She shoots him a silencing glare, and he scrambles
out of his seat.

"I'm sorry, Q." Ethan drags his fingers through his
hair, watching them walk away with a look of dismay. "I
didn't mean to ruin your big night."

"You didn't. Honestly. When Matt and Veronica
started being... well, their usual selves, I wished I never
agreed to this dinner and that we had stuck with whatever you had planned instead. So, in a way, *I'm* the one
who ruined the night by veering from the original
plans."

"It's not too late, you know." The corner of his
mouth lifts in a smile.

"But you already canceled your reservations."

"True. But the owner is a friend who insists on
doing me a favor since I built their website pro bono. So,
what do you say? Celebratory night do-over?"

"I'd like that."

As I watch Ethan explain the situation to Rowen,
and leave him with a generous tip, I'm once again struck
by how kind and thoughtful Ethan is, that even after the
disastrous events thus far, he's going out of his way to
make the night special. While I'm saddened by the way
things turned out with Matt and Veronica, I can't help
feeling like the evening is unfolding exactly as it should
—with me and Ethan, just the two of us, together. And a

not-so-small part of me is excited to find out where he plans on taking me.

But when we exit the cab in front of a bookstore in Brooklyn—a bookstore that is obviously closed—I'm left more clueless than before.

What on earth are we doing here?

23

Ethan skips up the short brick steps and knocks on the door, three raps in rapid succession. I don't know what he's expecting to happen. The Closed sign couldn't be clearer.

But to my surprise, the solid brass hinges squeak open. A young woman greets him with a wide, warm smile. "Ciao, Ethan. You made it."

"Thanks for squeezing us in again."

"My pleasure! Come in, come in." She ushers us past the threshold before locking the door behind us.

Once inside, I do a double take. The bookstore is bathed in soft, ambient light emanating from vintage Tiffany lampshades, each polished piece of stained glass glowing a different vibrant color. Flickering candles in crystal votives dot the heavy oak shelves, illuminating the supple leather bindings. I notice a diverse range of glossy contemporary covers, classic hardbacks, and a front table featuring famous Italian writers from centuries past.

But what strikes me the most isn't the fact that I've walked into every self-proclaimed bookworm's paradise. Although, I'm definitely awestruck. What really has me baffled is the smell. The familiar scent of printing paper, ink, and worn leather mingles with the most mouthwatering aroma of roasted garlic, aged Parmesan, and freshly baked focaccia bread. It's heavenly and wholly unexpected.

Bewildered, I glance at Ethan. He's grinning at me with a mixture of delight and excitement, like when you've given someone the perfect gift and can't wait for them to open it.

"Gabrielle, this is Quincy. Quincy, Gabrielle."

"Hi," I say shyly, feeling out of my element.

"It's a pleasure to meet you, Quincy. Welcome to Libro."

"Or," Ethan interjects, "as locals lovingly call it, Books & Bread."

Gabrielle laughs. "I'll have to share that with my father."

"How is the chef tonight?" Ethan asks, furthering my confusion. I can't seem to reconcile what I'm seeing with what I'm smelling.

"Experimenting, as always. But I think you'll be pleased with tonight's menu." She leads us down a narrow aisle with towering bookshelves on either side, and my eyes widen when I spot the small round tables tucked at the end of each row. Dreamy-eyed couples and intimate parties of four are bent over the most scrumptious-looking meals, deep in conversation as candlelight bounces off beautifully bound books, creating the most idyllic atmosphere I've ever seen.

Gabrielle pauses at the last stack. The sign overhead reads Poetry-Romance. My heart flutters. "I hope this is to your liking," Gabrielle tells Ethan, gesturing to the table set for two at the end of the row.

"It's perfect, Gabby. Thanks."

When she disappears behind a display of books, Ethan offers me his arm. "Signorina."

I hook my hand in the crook of his elbow, blinking against a sudden surge of emotion as he guides me to the table and pulls out my chair. To think, I almost missed this.

For the rest of the evening, I feel like I'm living in a dream. A surreal, otherworldly, utterly perfect dream. And I can't help drawing a comparison between Matt—who chose the trendiest restaurant in the city to celebrate—and Ethan—who chose the restaurant that was most likely to bring me joy.

After our meal, we walk arm in arm, enjoying the quiet cobblestoned streets and ruddy brick buildings painted in the dazzling lights of the city. Ethan halts our wandering in a neighborhood fondly dubbed Dumbo, which he explains stands for Down Under the Manhattan Bridge Overpass.

Standing on Washington Street between Front and

Water Streets, with Ethan's arm casually draped around my shoulders, I experience one of those out-of-body moments, when the edges of the world turn fuzzy, and time stands still. Framed by looming brownstones on either side, the sleek, steel lines of the Brooklyn Bridge glitter against the obsidian sky. It's the most beautiful sight I've ever beheld, made even more captivating by the company.

"Pretty, huh?" he murmurs.

"It's breathtaking."

"I come out here a lot to enjoy the view," he admits. "In fact, this is where I was standing when Brynn called to tell me you were coming to stay with us. Do you want to know what my first thought was?"

My breath catches, and I nod slowly, desperate for him to continue.

"I thought, *If you care about this girl even half as much as you used to, you need to tell her how you feel.*"

His words settle over me, light and ephemeral, like a whisper on a faint breeze. And yet, they somehow also hang heavy with implication, the kind of statement that could change the course of your life.

My chest cinches, aching for an answer as I ask with painful uncertainty, "And do you? Feel the same way?"

His response seems to take ages, and when he finally speaks, it's a crushing blow. "No, I don't."

I crumble beneath the weight of my disappointment, but Ethan turns me toward him, meeting my gaze as he sweeps aside a strand of my hair. "I care about you even more than before, more than I thought possible. You're unlike anyone I've ever met. You're funny, kind, unbelievably clever, beautiful, and brave. You, Quincy Carmichael, aren't simply long-term material. You're the forever I've been waiting for."

Just when I think I've ceased breathing for the rest of eternity, Ethan lowers his mouth to mine. There's no preamble to his kiss, no warm-up or warning. The second our lips meet, the spark is fierce, unapologetic, and pure, like the hottest flame, warming me from the inside out. I clutch his coat's lapel, not sure I can stand of my own volition.

I confess. I've thought about kissing Ethan Delaney many, *many* times in my life. But even in my wildest imaginings, it was never like this. Never so all-consuming, so momentous and weighty. I feel the cobblestone shift beneath our feet, marking the moment everything changed.

When our lips part, he presses his forehead to mine and whispers, "I lost you once. I won't let it happen again."

I don't speak. I can't. What can I say? What does he mean? My thoughts are a jumble. My feelings are even more so. I want to hold on to whatever is happening between us, but I'm afraid that a single thought spoken out loud may be our undoing. So, I simply cling to him, savoring even the smallest sensation.

"I used distance as an excuse once," he says softly,

his fingertips caressing my hair again. "But I can work from anywhere."

Startled, I meet his gaze. "You'd give up New York?"

"I don't see it as giving up New York so much as it's gaining *you* in my life."

"But..." I trail off, struggling to wrap my head around the enormity of what he's saying. "But New York is your home."

"I love this city. But at the risk of being too cliché, it's true what they say. Home is wherever you are." He flashes me his adorable lopsided smile—the one that's made my knees melt since we were teens—and gently cups the side of my face, his thumb trailing along my cheekbone. "In case I'm still not being clear. I love New York, Q. But I love you more."

He kisses me again, this time so tenderly, my toes curl inside my boots.

And as I surrender to his touch, I'm almost able to block out the haunting whisper in the back of my mind. The one that says, *If you promise him forever, you'll only break his heart.*

24

As I lie awake that night, the voice inside my head grows louder, strangling all the sweetness from my evening with Ethan until all that remains is my crushing self-doubt.

I shift onto my side, careful not to disturb Whiskers, who's asleep on my pillow. In the moonlight, the murky shadows look even more ominous, as if something might be lurking beyond the edges of what I can see. I shudder at the thought but can't close my eyes. That's when the visions start.

Restless, I roll onto my back and stare up at the ceiling. But the visions find me there, too.

I can see that hot, sticky summer day as if it were unfolding in real time. Chad and I had finished our street vendor popsicles and were content to wander around Central Park with no agenda or destination. We were simply enjoying each other's company. We always enjoyed each other's company. Although we'd only been dating for six months, I had a feeling Chad was "the one." He made me feel fun, desirable, and worthy of love. It was a feeling I could get used to, and when the time came, I was prepared to give him my heart, wholly and completely, until death do us part.

Which is why, when he dropped to one knee at the center of the Gapstow Bridge, I thought my whole world was about to change for the better.

That's when I saw it. A shiny flash of metal.

My heart stopped. Both hands flew to my mouth, and I was barely able to contain an exhilarated "Yes!" from escaping my lips before Chad had a chance to pop the question.

But it wasn't an engagement ring.

"Look! A lucky penny." Chad pinched the small one-cent piece between his fingertips as if he'd found buried treasure.

Shame swept across my face, heating my cheeks more than the late afternoon sunlight. I tried to recover quickly, but traitorous tears pricked my eyes, threatening to reveal my humiliating miscalculation.

"What's wrong?" he'd asked.

I'd rushed to assure him that nothing was wrong, but the waver in my voice gave me away.

"What is it?" he'd pressed. "Just tell me."

I'd gathered the muggy air in one long, fortifying breath, telling myself that my blunder was humorous, a case of misplaced expectations that we could laugh about together.

But even now, over ten years later, I know there was nothing funny about that moment. And the heat of humiliation still burns in my chest. I force my eyes open, my gaze pinned on a sinewy crack in the plaster overhead, willing the images of that day into disjointed, cloudy images.

A hot tear slips from the corner of my eye, leaving a scalding trail along the side of my face before dampening the pillowcase.

Chad had stood, tucking the penny into his pocket as he leaned against the stone wall, waiting for me to explain. Sunlight had gleamed off his sandy-brown hair, making it appear golden against his tanned skin. He'd worn it longer then. Floppy, as my mother described it. The strands had fanned against his neck, giving him a perpetual boyish look. I used to love twisting my fingertips into the curled ends.

"It's nothing," I'd repeated, trying to sound casual. "I thought that maybe... when you got down on one knee and everything..." I'd trailed off, losing my nerve.

But he'd caught on, his eyes widening in shock. "You thought I was going to propose?" He sounded so astonished his reaction bordered on appalled.

I was instantly mortified.

"Sorry, Quincy," he'd said hastily. "I didn't mean to sound so surprised. I just... Well, I thought we were on the same page."

"And what page is that?" I'd asked meekly, terrified of the answer.

"You know." He'd dug both hands in his pockets, looking like he'd rather jump off the bridge than have this conversation. "That we're just having fun. A temporary thing. I mean, you're a great girl. But you're not exactly the marriage type."

"I—I'm not?" My throat had felt raw, as if the words had clawed their way out. I knew I wasn't the obvious choice for someone's wife. I couldn't cook to save my life and was admittedly hopeless when it came to anything domestic. I'd tried to fold one of those fitted sheets once, and nearly pulled a muscle. But this wasn't the 1950s anymore. Surely he hadn't ruled me out on that criteria alone.

"Look, Quincy." He'd sighed so deeply, his shoulders had slumped forward, making him appear small and defeated for the first time since I'd known him. "My parents are divorced. I've seen what it does to a family. When I get married, I want it to be for the long haul. I'm talking about a forever kind of deal."

I remember nodding vigorously, desperate to show him that I felt the same way. But it didn't matter. Not when he'd said what came next.

"Marriage takes work," he'd told me, as if I might not have realized that nuptial tidbit. "You can't quit when it gets hard." He'd met my gaze with a pained, almost apologetic look and said softly, "I care about you, Quincy. But you're not long-term material."

Although spoken with something akin to kindness, I'd felt like I'd been slapped across the face. My eyes had stung and watered, my breath escaped me. Every fiber in my being had ached. And yet, I didn't have a comeback. Chad was right. I did quit everything I started, especially when things didn't go my way. Did I really think I had what it took to make a marriage last a lifetime?

You're the forever I've been waiting for.

Ethan's words from earlier that evening found their way into the forefront of my mind.

Forever.

Ethan was willing to give up New York... Brynn, Wilson, everything he loved and cared about. For me. But what if Chad was right? What if I let Ethan uproot his entire life only to abandon him the second things got hard?

I don't think I could live with myself.

Once, when I was working on an ad campaign for nicotine gum, I did some research on addiction. I remember reading that sometimes the most caring thing an addict can do for their loved ones is to extricate themselves from their lives until they get the help they need. Otherwise, you could risk dragging them down with you.

This is the rationale I repeat over and over as I book a return flight, pack my bag, and slip Whiskers into her cat carrier.

But it's strange. You know what else I remember

from my research? Addicts are masterful at rationalizing their behavior. They can put a spin on almost anything, including making the most selfish, fear-based decision sound sacrificial. But I don't dwell on this particular bit of knowledge, even as my boots *click-clack* accusingly across the hardwood floor.

I set my phone on Whiskers's carrier so I can easily see the notification that my Uber has arrived, then cast one final glance around the apartment I'd called home, tears obscuring my vision. But when I reach for the doorknob, my fingers curl back. I can't bring myself to grip the cool metal, no matter how many times I tell myself it's for the greater good.

"I can't believe you're running away again." Brynn's pained whisper comes from behind me, and when I turn toward the sound, my heart wrenches at the glimmer of intense sorrow and disappointment in her eyes. "I thought things might be different this time."

"Brynn, I—" I attempt to offer an explanation, but there isn't one. I suddenly feel ashamed and confused and so very weary. A wiser, more mature voice in my head whispers I should have waited until morning. Things always look brighter when the sunlight chases away the shadows.

"Save your excuses, Quincy. I've heard them all before." Her words are harsh but true. And I can't blame her. "This is why I didn't want you dating Ethan. I couldn't bear the possibility that you'd break his heart. But then I thought maybe you were different. Maybe you're not the same Quincy who quits the second life gets tough or a little messy."

I wince, forced to face my own self-fulfilling prophecy.

"But I was wrong." Her voice trembles now, twinged with the kind of bitterness born from betrayal. "You're exactly the same as you always were."

Never has a single sentence, so simple on the surface, stung so sharply. And while the sentiment couldn't be more deserved, I can't help feeling defensive.

"Are we really so dissimilar?" I murmur, surprising my own ears.

"What?" Her hurt momentarily gives way to her shock.

"Aren't you afraid to go out with Oliver? You're so worried you'll wind up like your parents, you won't even give him a chance."

"That's different," she snaps.

"Is it?" I press, though I should really stop talking now. I'm only making an awful situation so much worse. "You're living your life in fear exactly like I am, choosing to believe the worst-case scenario instead of choosing hope. Because fear is easier. Fear is comfortable. Fear is the friend that says they want the best for you, but you know it's a lie." The words spill out of me, and I can't stop them. I'm not even sure if they make sense, but I don't want tonight to end with each of us saying things we'll regret. Things we can't take back. I need to change course before it's too late.

At this moment, right now, I have a choice. I can live my life according to my track record, believing I'll continue to behave how I always have. Or I can choose the other option. The riskier, more terrifying, possibly disastrous one.

But the big, potentially life-altering question is am I brave enough?

Before I can decide, my phone buzzes.

I instinctively glance at the screen and my blood chills, stilling in my veins.

It's a group message from my mom. And even in the simple, straightforward text, I can hear her quiet desperation.

> How soon can you kids get home?
> Your father had a heart attack.

25

The man lying in the hospital bed doesn't look like my father. My father is strong and striking, able to command a room simply by walking through the doorway. This man—the one in the stiff, papery gown with gaunt features and glassy eyes—looks frail and worn, a faded image of my father's vibrant vitality. But he's alive. And for that, I'm grateful.

From the second I left Brynn's apartment—in shock and mumbling that I had to leave—I haven't been able to think about anything other than preparing myself for the worst. I haven't thought about what to say to Ethan, or how to fix things with Brynn. My thoughts kept circling back to the same gut-wrenching questions. What if I'm too late? What if Dad's gone before I get there? What if I never hear his voice again? Or smell his aftershave? Or stretch onto my tiptoes to kiss his cheek?

Seeing him now as I peer around the privacy

curtain, watching Mom fuss over imaginary wrinkles in the flimsy cotton sheets, I feel like I'm trapped in a nightmare. The kind where I'm being chased, but my legs don't work, and no matter how hard I try, I can't wake up.

My throat tingles, a telltale sign of impending tears, and I cough as quietly as I can, but my mom glances up and catches my eye. Without a word, she rushes into my arms, clinging to me so tightly, my heart breaks. "I'm so glad you're here," she whispers against my hair, and it occurs to me that my mother—the most composed person I know—is looking to me for comfort. The realization is all the more sobering.

"How is he?" I ask, even though he's awake, alert, and can speak for himself.

"Stubborn as ever," she says, pulling back to smooth her flyaways. "Trying to tell the doctors how to do their jobs."

"Is it my fault I know more about modern medicine than these premed students masquerading as medical professionals?"

"Watching every episode of *House* and *General Hospital* doesn't make you an expert." Mom rolls her eyes, but I can tell she's trying not to cry. She summons a smile. "Well, I'll let you two visit and pop down to the cafeteria for a bit. Can I get you anything?"

"No thanks," I say.

"I'd kill for an espresso," Dad chimes in.

"You mean an espresso would kill you," Mom

corrects, then turns to me with an exasperated wave of her hand. "See what I have to deal with?" She casts a loving glance at my father before slipping out of the room, leaving us alone.

"She means well." Dad manages a grin, but it accentuates the lines of exhaustion around his eyes. "I'm glad you're here." He gestures to the empty seat by his bedside. "Did you enjoy your time in New York?"

"I did," I say honestly and without hesitation.

"But it's good to be back." It sounds more like a statement than a question.

"Yes," I answer after a pause, even though I have mixed feelings on the subject. "But the circumstances could be better," I add, aiming for some levity.

"Amen to that. But tell me. How does it feel to finish a decade's worth of Christmas Commitments?"

"Technically, I still have one left," I admit, praying he doesn't ask what it is. Although I've regularly reported on my progress, I'm not surprised the final task fell through the cracks as he's kept count. I've done my best to avoid mentioning it. Honestly, I don't know what I was thinking when I wrote it down. I certainly didn't consider how it would play out when I finally had to reveal what I'd chosen. But in the moment, it had gripped me with such intense urgency, I couldn't think of anything else.

"Well," he quips, "nine out of ten is close enough."

"What do you mean? Close enough for what?"

"I mean," he says with dramatic emphasis. "I want

you to take over as the new marketing director. Effective immediately."

He's staring at me intently, waiting for my response, but I merely gape at him for what feels like five full minutes while his heart monitor beeps impatiently. Finally, I mumble, "B-but I didn't finish the list."

"That may be true, but I make the rules, so I'm allowed to break them." He chuckles, but it sounds raspy and weak. Not at all like his usual robust laugh. "Extra Energy Drink loved your proposal. They want you to implement it right away. And given the circumstances"—he waves a hand over his prone body—"I'm going to need a new right-hand man—or *woman*, I should say—sooner than I thought. Congratulations. I'm proud of you, kiddo."

He lays a hand on my shoulder, and apart from all the protruding tubes and wires, this moment is exactly how I'd always envisioned it would be—my father smiling in a soft, understated way as he says the four words I've waited my whole life to hear. The words that mark the completion of my Christmas Commitments.

Make Dad proud.

I can finally cross off the final task.

Part of me doesn't believe it. And I consider asking if he'll say the words again, to make sure I hadn't blacked out and imagined them. But I don't get the chance.

"Knock, knock." Matt sweeps aside the curtain and steps inside, followed by Veronica.

At first, I hardly recognize her. My perpetually put-together sister looks rumpled and unkempt, her hair a tangled mess, her eyes red and puffy. There's even smeared mascara below her lash line that she hasn't bothered to fix.

"How are you doing, Dad?" Matt asks, coming to stand by his bedside.

"Better now that all my kids are here."

"What do the doctors say?" Veronica's voice is strained with worry, and she unsuccessfully hides a sniffle behind her sleeve.

"That I need to slow down and take things easy."

"We'll help," she offers quickly. "We can each take on more responsibility at work."

"About that..." Dad squeezes my shoulder. "I've asked your sister to take over Steve Bailcroft's position. She really knocked it out of the park with her Extra pitch. You two should see it." He points to his laptop on the side table. "Hand me that, would you, Matt?"

As my brother grabs the laptop, my pulse sputters, and I barely stop myself from lunging at him and snatching it from his hand. Although I know the campaign has already surpassed my father's expectations—and secured me the coveted promotion—I can't help revisiting every miserable moment in my childhood when my work was put on display only to be ridiculed.

I briefly close my eyes, trying to ground myself in the knowledge that their opinions don't define me. My campaign is good, and I don't need their acknowledgment for those words to be true. As my eyes flicker open, the video I created for Extra Energy Drink is showcased on the screen. The action shots of men and women accomplishing extraordinary feats are familiar. So is the slogan. *When you feel like giving up, don't quit. Just take a sip.* The stock video clip shows an image of a runner, sweaty and exhausted, taking a sip from a plain soda can—on which I superimposed Extra Energy Drink's logo—before bursting across the finish line, her strained features giving way to triumph and euphoria.

I smile, recalling the exact moment the slogan sprang to mind, sparked by something Ethan had said. *Ethan...* A sharp twinge stabs my chest, and I attempt to focus on anything other than the pain. I divert my attention to my father's face, amazed by the unbridled admiration sprawled across it. It's a look I've seen before but never aimed at me. "Well, what do you think?" he asks my siblings, who've remarkably remained quiet through the entire commercial.

"Wow." Matt whistles. "It's impressive. Congratulations, Quince. You deserve the win." He sounds so sincere, and I can't help contrasting this moment with our fight less than twenty-four hours ago. It's as if our shared concern over Dad's condition erased it from our collective memory.

Veronica glances in my direction, and maybe it's due to her disheveled appearance, but I can't read her expression. She turns back to Dad and says, "The campaign is great. And if you think Quincy is the best one for the job, we'll do whatever we can to make it a smooth transition."

"Thanks, sweetheart." The warm pressure of his palm leaves my shoulder as he reaches for her hand. "I knew you kids would work things out together. I was just telling your mother I don't know what I'd do without you three."

A few months ago, this moment would've meant everything to me. Not only winning my father's approval but securing his confidence. To think, he's essentially put me in charge during his recovery. He's actually counting on *me*, the eternally unreliable. The scenario seems so far-fetched, I'm tempted to pinch myself. This is everything I've ever wanted.

At least, it used to be.

But now, I can't help thinking about Brynn and Ethan. I abandoned them without an explanation, left without a goodbye. And Whiskers is in my apartment right now, alone in an unfamiliar place.

I should be overjoyed that I've finally made my father proud and left behind the moniker that has haunted me my entire life. I'm no longer Quincy the Quitter, the missing link in my family of overachievers. But at what cost? Now there are other people in my life who are important to me, who I care for deeply, and I've let them down.

What's worse? I don't know if I can ever make it up to them.

26

Since the doctors want to observe Dad for a few more days, we've been taking turns at the hospital. This afternoon is Matt's shift, so I'm free to go on my fool's errand—trying to locate my camp trinkets from when we were kids. I don't know why, but I'm desperate to find the friendship bracelet Brynn made for me, the one with green and purple thread dotted with tiny pink beads. I'm also searching for the matching tie-dyed T-shirt we stamped with our handprints, although I doubt it will still fit me.

I shove aside another dusty box, sighing in frustration. I've dug through half of our garage already with no luck. But why my parents felt the need to save so many pairs of bell-bottoms, I'll never know. "This may be a big waste of time," I tell Whiskers, who's wreaking havoc in a large cardboard box filled with my old, lumpy stuffed animals so I can keep tabs on her. I've already noticed several missing eyes and torn limbs, but I'm experiencing a strong bout of "mom guilt" for taking her from Wilson, so I let her have her fun, no matter how sadistic it might seem.

Wilson... The image of his sweet, fluffy face twists the knot in my stomach even tighter. I've tried to avoid thinking about him until I make a decision about my future. I've also avoided texts and voice mails from Brynn and Ethan for the same reason. Honestly, it's been torture. I'm fairly certain if someone were to look up The Worst Person in the World in the dictionary, they'd see my photo.

But I have no idea what I'd even say to them. How can I tell them that the one thing I want more than anything is to be back in New York, with them, but I'm not sure I can leave my family. Not now. Not when they finally need me.

"Quincy? Are you in here?" Veronica trips over a stack of open boxes, spilling the contents. Matt's high school gym clothes litter the concrete floor, and she wrinkles her nose. "Ew. Is that a jockstrap?"

"Sadly, not the grossest thing I've found out here." I cringe, recalling the ancient retainer that had a rather disturbing odor.

"What are you looking for?" She surveys the barricade of boxes, both hands on her slim hips. Dressed in her Lululemon leggings and a long cashmere sweater—not to mention her sleek ponytail without a single stray hair—she looks more like herself today.

"Just a few things from camp."

"Why?"

I hesitate, wondering how to explain it when I barely understand my motivation myself.

She seems to sense that it's a weighty topic and holds up her hand. "Never mind. Don't tell me."

"Did you need something?" I lift an old soccer jersey out of the box, realizing that while I wouldn't normally choose her company, I'm grateful for the distraction from my plaguing thoughts.

"Who played soccer?" she asks.

"I did."

"Strange. I don't remember that."

"I don't see why you would," I say with a shrug. "You never came to any of the games. And I didn't even last a full season."

"I don't blame you. Not when the uniforms are this tacky." She pulls a face at the shimmery polyester fabric, then her gaze falls on a faded playbill. "Wait. You were in *The Wizard of Oz*?"

"Sophomore year. I was supposed to be the Tin Man but dropped out before opening night." I don't mention it's partially because she caught me practicing my lines and told me that all the oil cans in the world couldn't save my stiff performance.

She stares at the playbill, turning it over in her hand as if she'd never seen one before, and I can't help wondering what she's doing here. She didn't come out to our garage to take a morbid trip down memory lane.

"I owe you an apology."

I blink in bewilderment. What did she say? I'm unable to recall a single time my sister apologized for anything. At least, not without parental insistence and under duress. And for years, I've overlooked her poor behavior, letting it slide as her spitefulness slowly eroded our relationship even further. But maybe she's not the only one to blame. Maybe it's time I tell her exactly how I feel.

"Yes," I whisper, my voice a tenuous tremor. "You do."

Now, it's her turn to be surprised. "What?"

"Ethan wasn't wrong, you know," I say, gaining courage simply by evoking his name. "All I've ever wanted was your respect and friendship, to feel like you cared about me. There have been moments of kindness, sprinkled here and there, but overall, you haven't exactly been a model big sister."

Tears fill her eyes, collecting in her lashes like tiny dewdrops before tumbling down her cheeks. "You're right. And so was Ethan. I've been a jealous jerk."

I'm fairly certain my mouth has literally fallen open in shock. I expected her to protest or deflect, not agree with me.

"I grew up in Matt's shadow," she continues softly, fidgeting with the crisp paper folds of the playbill. "He was the firstborn son. The golden child. Everything came so easily to him. But not me. I had to fight for every second of attention, every word of affection, every sliver of praise. Then you came along." Her voice quivers, tears puddling in her eyes again, making them appear twice their normal size. She always was a pretty crier.

"You were the precious baby of the family. The happy surprise. Mom and Dad adored you. And I was so afraid you'd take my place. That I'd go from being second best to completely forgotten."

As she stands before me, her cheeks pale and damp, her nose red, I've never seen her look so vulnerable. She's no longer my perfect sibling, the one on a pedestal, looking down on us little people. She's a real person, with fears and flaws, just like me. And strangely, I've never respected her more.

"The truth is," she says sorrowfully, "I'm ashamed of how I've treated you. As the older sister, it was my job to look out for you. I should've helped you find your way in this crazy, competitive family of ours. Instead, I did the opposite. I tore you down every chance I got, hoping to make myself look better. Except, it didn't make me look better. It made me look petty. And ugly. And small." She sniffles, attempting a smile. "You may not believe me, but I've secretly admired you, Quincy. Because somehow, even with subpar siblings like me and Matt, you never got bitter. You're kind and generous and forgiving. Even when we don't deserve it. And trust me, I know we don't deserve it."

"I—I don't know what to say." Tears blur my own vision now, and I desperately want to hug her, but I don't know how she'll react. This moment is too precious, too precarious. I don't want to risk ruining it, even for a second.

"You don't have to say anything. I just wanted to apologize. And tell you that, while it might be too late, I'm going to try and be the big sister I should've been when we were growing up."

Too emotional to speak, I blow my nose into my soccer jersey, reasoning that I'll probably throw it away later, anyway. All of a sudden, I have a vision of me and Veronica shopping Rodeo Drive, laughing over low-fat lattes as we try on different outfits, modeling them for each other in a movie-like montage. Could this really be the beginning of an honest-to-goodness relationship? Like the kind I've read about in all those women's fiction novels? It doesn't seem possible, but it's also not the first miracle I've witnessed lately.

"My first act as your new and improved big sister is to tell you this," Veronica says, setting the playbill back in the box. "Whether you take the promotion or not, don't throw away what you have with Ethan. I've waited my whole life for someone to love me the way that man loves you. And whatever it takes to hold on to him—long distance, relocating, *whatever*—do it." Her features soften, her lips curling ever so slightly into a smile. "When I saw you and Ethan at the marathon, I could instantly tell that what you two have is special. He's the kind of man who loves you exactly as you are but will do anything and everything to help you become the best version of yourself. Do you understand how rare that is?"

"I do," I whisper, suddenly missing Ethan so much it hurts. I've been such a coward, compartmentalizing my life because of my indecision and fear. But Ethan—and Brynn—deserve to know what's going on, even if I don't have a clear answer yet.

"Then what's wrong?" Veronica asks, sensing my internal torment.

"I—I think I've messed things up."

"Then let's figure out how you're going to fix them."

To my surprise, she maneuvers around the stack of boxes and pulls me into a hug. Her embrace is awkward at first, her arms stiff, her posture rigid. But as I melt against her, I feel her body relax, and for the first time since I left New York, I wonder if maybe... just maybe... everything will turn out okay after all.

27

Part of me isn't surprised to find my dad hard at work, even in his hospital bed. "Aren't you supposed to be resting?" I ask, trying to sound stern and disapproving, although it's difficult when he looks so content.

The incline of his bed is elevated as upright as it will go, and the table—which is supposed to be reserved for pills and pudding cups—is engulfed by two open laptops. Okay, and one empty pudding cup. Chocolate, from the looks of it.

"I *am* resting," he insists with a wry grin. "I tried to convince your mother to bring my large monitor from the office and replace the TV with it, but she felt that was going too far. So, here we are." Still grinning, he waves a hand over his tandem laptops.

He finally has some color back in his face, and according to Mom, he'll be discharged soon. This should be a time of rejoicing. But instead, I'm the bearer of bad news. *Really* bad news. In hindsight, I should've brought some chocolate—or bourbon—to soften the blow.

My throat tightens, and I try to swallow but suddenly forget how. In a flash of panic, I wrap my fingers around my neck. This is how I'm going to die— by drowning in my own drool because my God-given reflex is on the fritz.

"Are you okay?" Dad gives me a funny look, and I lower my hands, thankfully able to swallow again, although it goes down the wrong tube.

"Uh-huh," I sputter and cough, definitely *not* okay. And not only because I'm choking on my saliva. I still can't believe I waited my whole life to hear my father say he's proud of me, and now that he finally has, I'm about to hit the Undo button. And not only that, I'm about to abandon him—and the company—in his time of need. What kind of daughter am I?

"Have a seat." He gestures to the stiff armchair by his bedside. "I want to go over some of the current accounts with you. I know you'll primarily be focused on Extra Energy Drink, but there are a few others that will need your immediate attention, Miss Marketing Director." Guilt pumps through my veins like gasoline, and his jovial teasing is like a lit match. I'm fairly certain I'm seconds away from internal combustion. Maybe I can't do this....

I gather a breath, mentally revisiting my conversation with Veronica, which, admittedly, is a strange feeling. The only thing more surreal than listening to my sister's advice is actually taking it. But this time, I think she's right.

"About that, Dad." The vinyl cushion squeaks as I shift my weight. But I think my discomfort has less to do with the poorly constructed seating—which seems purposefully designed to be as uncomfortable as possible—and everything to do with the fact that my life is about to implode.

"Uh-oh. Don't tell me. You want a bigger budget to redecorate Steve's office?" He laughs, but immediately sobers when I don't join in. "What's on your mind, kiddo?"

Kiddo. Somehow, my father is able to make me feel like a respected business professional *and* his little girl all at the same time. A poignant combination that makes what I'm about to do so much harder than I anticipated. Which is saying a lot, since I already equated it to stabbing needles underneath my fingernails.

He imperceptibly leans forward, waiting for my response, but I can't speak. Tears sting my eyes, and my pulse quickens with apprehension. For a moment, I contemplate utilizing the Lamaze-style breathing I saw a pregnant woman performing in the elevator when I arrived. Although I'm not sure why. It didn't seem to alleviate her anxiety, and I wonder if my eyes hold the same spark of trepidation. Not that I consider my situation to be the same level of trauma as childbirth or anything.

"It can't be that bad," Dad says, as if he can read my mind.

"I'm afraid it is." I wring my hands, wishing I could fast-forward to some point in time after this conversation. "I have something I need to tell you, but I'm not sure how."

"You can tell me anything."

"Can I?" I ask tearfully. "Can I tell you that the daughter you're finally proud of is as unreliable as ever? That I haven't changed at all?" The words tumble out of me in a rush of verbal anguish, and my father peers at me with concern and confusion.

"What are you talking about, sweetheart?"

"I can't accept the promotion. And I... I... I quit," I say in a strangled sob, burying my face in my hands.

He's silent for a long, agonizing moment. So long, I'm tempted to peek through my fingertips, but I know I won't be able to bear his look of disappointment.

"May I ask why?" he asks quietly.

"Because I have to go home. To New York. It's where I belong, Dad. I'll stay in California long enough to finish up with the energy drink account, but then I have to go back. I'm so, so sorry. I know I'm letting you down again. I guess it's just who I am. Quincy the Quitter." The nickname tastes bitter on my tongue, but it's never felt more fitting. It seems no matter how hard I try, I'm destined to disappoint someone—Brynn, Ethan, my dad, even myself. Maybe it's time I face it.

I lift my head, meeting my father's gaze. I expect displeasure. Maybe even reproach or regret. Instead, his gaze is soft and tender, shimmering with a depth of affection I've never seen before.

"Don't be sorry. And don't call yourself a quitter." He closes both laptop screens, turning slightly to face me, making sure he has my full attention. "Sure, you quit things. More things than you probably should. But I suspect that's my fault. I wanted to instill drive, ambition, and friendly competition, but I might've gone too far, teaching you that something isn't worth doing unless you can be the best. If this *blip*," he says, gesturing to his hospital bed, "has taught me anything, it's that I might have an unhealthy pursuit of perfection. Which I passed on to you kids." Leaning forward, he holds my gaze with intent and purpose, and I blink back my tears, wanting to memorize every line and crease of his face, immortalizing this moment. "But I want you to know this, kiddo, without a shadow of a doubt. When it comes to the things that matter—like loving this family —you are *not* a quitter. You never give up on us, even when we make it difficult. And when it comes time for you to have your own family, I know you'll love them just as fiercely and unwaveringly as you do ours. And that, sweetheart, is one of the many reasons you've *always* made me proud."

His words wash over me like a cool, refreshing balm,

healing both heart and soul. My whole life, I'd strived for outward approval, trying desperately to be what I thought everyone else expected, instead of realizing I had gifts of my own. Gifts that, while different and unique to me, are just as valuable. Why hadn't I realized that before? Springing from my seat, I throw my arms around his neck, inhaling the strange, musky scent of expensive cologne mixed with medicated salve and bleached bedding.

Like most people, I've never been a fan of hospitals. But after today, they may be one of my new favorite places. That is, after New York. The city that holds my heart. The city that's calling me back home.

"Careful," Dad says, chuckling softly. "I think your hand is caught in my IV." Of course, we both know it's not, but ill-timed jokes have always been his love language. The same way Ethan's is food and Brynn's is a sensible budget.

"Love you, too, Dad," I say, smiling through my tears. Only this time, they're happy tears.

"One more thing," he adds, taking on a more serious tone.

"What's that?"

"I have a proposition for you. And before you say no, hear me out."

"Okay," I say slowly, curious what he has in mind.

But nothing could prepare me for what came next.

28

The overzealous cab driver veers around a wayward pedestrian, slamming my head against the window. I groan, gripping the sore spot, but my smile doesn't fade. How could it? I'm back home. In the city that never sleeps. Because who wants to sleep when you're in a place this spectacular?

I've already dropped my bags off in the lobby of Brynn's apartment building and asked Sharon, the doorman—door *person*?—to watch Whiskers for me, since she said neither Ethan nor Brynn were home. I'd considered letting myself inside with the key I'd never given back, but I didn't want to presume, especially since Brynn and I technically haven't spoken since our fight before I left.

Of course, I realize that showing up unannounced at her place of employment is a risky move. And I fully accept that my choice in attire will lead to a healthy dose of public humiliation. But I honestly don't care. It's time for the grand gesture, like in every romantic comedy I've ever watched. Except, in this scenario, I'm not winning back my leading man. Not yet, anyway. This time, I'm wooing my best friend. Let's just hope this story has a happy ending.

I hop out of the cab and immediately garner several sneering glances. Admittedly, my T-shirt is a bit too tight and a little too short. And the poorly placed hand-prints are borderline inappropriate now that I've passed puberty. But still, haven't New Yorkers seen worse than my tacky tie-dyed tee from camp?

Ignoring the raised eyebrows, I push through the revolving front door and make a beeline for the lobby receptionist.

"Can I help you?" She frowns at the palm prints on my chest, and I'm tempted to say, "Hey, lady, my eyes are up here." Instead, I manage a smile. "The offices of Richmond and Fairfax Financials, please."

Her eyes widen in surprise, and I'm guessing I'm not their usual clientele. "Um, eighth floor."

"Thank you." I endure an awkward elevator ride with two men in slick suits who seem to think their stares are subtle. To block their view, I cross my arms in front of my chest, even though the action brings my shoulders up to my ears. When the doors slide open, I dash out as quickly as if the cables had just been cut and the giant metal box was about to plummet into oblivion.

Lifting my chin, I stride into Richmond and Fairfax Financials with as much self-confidence as I can muster given the circumstances. Brynn's workplace is as glossy and glamorous as I'd imagined—all white, crisp, and polished to perfection, without a single paper clip out of place. And the staff looks sleek and sophisticated, the epitome of New York City professionalism—aka the exact opposite of my appearance at the moment.

The slender, impeccably dressed receptionist plasters on a polite smile when I approach her pristine desk. "Hello. Do you have an appointment?"

"Uh, not exactly. I'm here to see Brynn Delaney."

"Oh." She looks disappointed, like she'd expected me to admit I'd just woken up from a twenty-year coma and accidentally wandered into their building. "I'm sorry. She just left."

My face falls, and for some reason, she takes pity on me—the poor, fashion-challenged amnesiac—and adds, "But she's only one floor up, at the coffee cart on the terrace. You can probably catch her there."

"Thank you, thank you!" I gush before rushing back to the elevator.

Thankfully, I'm alone this time and enjoy the thirty second gawk-free zone until the doors open on the next floor, revealing the fanciest looking cafeteria I've ever seen. Through a long wall of windows, I spot the terrace —a large outdoor space with cozy seating and a breathtaking view of the city. There's a coffee cart stationed near the stone perimeter, and as I approach, I spot

Brynn pouring a sugar packet into a paper cup. Oliver stands beside her, one hand on the small of her back as he leans in to whisper something in her ear.

I instantly freeze, mesmerized by the startling exchange. I wait for Brynn to pull away and shirk off his hand, but she laughs softly, gazing up at him with an expression of open affection. There's an undeniable intimacy between them that transcends the bond of coworkers, even friendship, and I'm stunned into a silent stupor. Obviously, I missed something monumental in the handful of days I was back in LA, and my heart sinks with regret.

As they move away from the cart with their coffee—Oliver's hand still poised on Brynn's lower back—she catches my eye. For a moment, neither of us moves, speaks, or even blinks. We simply stare like a couple of jaywalkers caught in a cabbie's headlights.

Finally, she asks in bewilderment, "Quincy? What are you doing here?" Her baffled gaze travels over my T-shirt, landing on my wrist as I nervously tuck a strand of hair behind my ear. There's a spark of recognition in her dark eyes when she notices the bracelet. Her gaze locks on mine, questioning.

"I'm here to say what I should have said ten years ago." I gather a breath, valiantly ignoring the ogling onlookers. "I'm sorry for not joining you in New York all those years ago like I'd promised. I'm sorry I let our friendship fizzle, as if it didn't matter to me. As if *you* didn't matter to me." My voice trembles, but I keep going. "The truth is, you've always been like a sister to me. The kind of sister I always wanted. Loving, supportive, and patient with all my faults. But I took you for granted. And I let you down, more times than I can count. I know I don't deserve a second chance. Or a third. But I went too long without you in my life, and I can't go back to a Brynn-less existence."

The words spill out of me like a wellspring of thoughts and emotions that have gone unspoken for far too long. And while they're heartfelt, I'm not entirely sure they're coherent. To be honest, the whole scene is a bit of a blur, and before I realize what I'm doing, I drop down on one knee, clearly influenced by binge-watching too many Hallmark movies.

Brynn and Oliver—and the entire terrace of transfixed spectators—gape at me, but I've come too far to turn back now.

I slip the bracelet off my wrist and offer it to her like some sort of odd, oversized engagement ring. "Brynn Rose Delaney, will you do me the honor of being my best friend forever? Until death do us part?"

In the wake of my peculiar platonic proposal, the early spring air turns eerily silent, save for a single bird whose lilting twitter almost sounds like it's laughing at me. I tune it out, intent on Brynn's reaction.

A string of emotions flickers across her face as she processes my bizarre behavior.

I hold my breath, suddenly understanding how a man must feel when he pours out his heart, putting it on display to either be received or rejected for the entire world to watch.

After what seems like an eternity, Brynn steps forward and tearfully plucks the bracelet from my gasp. "Yes! Of course I will, you big goofball. Best friends forever."

She slips the bracelet over her wrist, and I jump to my feet, gathering her in a bone-crushing hug while our befuddled audience applauds with the kind of disjointed cadence that betrays their confusion.

When we break apart, Brynn is grinning broadly. "If this is your apology to me, I can't wait to see what you have planned for Ethan," she teases.

My stomach flutters at the thought of seeing him again. I've missed his slanted smile, the silky smooth thrum of his voice, the way his presence simultaneously puts me at ease and makes my skin tingle with excitement. "Do you know where he is?"

"He's meeting with potential investors for MAD Market."

My heart swells, and I'm so thrilled for him, I think it might actually burst. But I'd promised to be there. "Do you know where?"

"I do, why?"

"Because I've missed too many important moments already. Which reminds me, I want to hear about all of *this*," I say, wagging my finger between her and Oliver.

Brynn blushes. "Let's just say you were right."

"I need details. But first, I need the address for

Ethan's meeting." I spin on my heel, ready to march off as soon as I know where I'm headed.

"Wait, Quincy." Brynn grabs my hand. "I don't think that's such a good idea."

"You don't?" My spirits falter as I meet her gaze, suddenly teetering between hope and apprehension.

Her lips quirk as she eyes my wardrobe. "We might need to do something about that T-shirt first."

29

As I ride the elevator to the fifteenth floor—in a building not too far from Brynn's—I tug on the hem of her pinstriped suit jacket. While it might be a bit snug, it covers most of my torso (including the conspicuous handprints), and I'm grateful she suggested I borrow it. Her pants, on the other hand, hit above my ankles, so I'm stuck with my lightweight linen trousers. Fortunately, I saw an article in *Vogue* recently where similar bottoms were paired with a blazer for a "laid-back office look," and I'm hopeful I can pull it off.

To my delight, the receptionist actually compliments my outfit, and doesn't even bat an eyelash when I recite my rehearsed speech, escorting me to the conference room without a single question asked. So far, this is playing out perfectly. Although, it could still devolve into a disaster. I have no idea how Ethan will react when he sees me.

He does a double take when I stride into the room, then his shoulders visibly relax with relief. His nervous energy is palpable, and I know exactly how he feels. The first time I pitched an ad campaign was for a dog treat company, and I was so racked with anxiety, I nervously took a bite out of a bacon-flavored biscuit. I tried to play it off as part of my presentation—dog treats so *paw*sitively delicious, they're not just for pets—but I'm not sure they were convinced. I did land the account, though.

"Sorry I'm late." I set Brynn's briefcase on the long conference table and whip out her laptop. Thankfully, everything I need is cloud-based.

"And *you* are?" A middle-aged man in a steel-gray suit narrows his gaze at me, and his two subordinates—who look like slightly younger carbon copies—follow his lead.

"Quincy Carmichael, CEO of Carmichael Creatives, East Coast Division." I flip open the laptop, getting a thrill out of saying my new job title for the first time. "I'm personally handling all of MAD Market's advertising needs."

"You didn't mention you were already working with a marketing firm." Steel Suit turns to Ethan, sounding impressed.

Ethan opens his mouth but is still too stunned to speak.

"Not only that," I add, giving him time to recover from my unexpected entrance. "We already have our first ad campaign." I pull up the video I showed Ethan several weeks ago and press Play, reveling in the way their expressions brighten with increased interest as each new celebrity appears on screen. I can already tell they're hooked, but for good measure, I wait until the end of the video and say casually, "Two of the celebrities you saw in this video have already agreed to come on board as investors. So, if you want to get in on the ground floor, I suggest you act quickly."

I can barely refrain from laughing as they exchange glances, practically salivating with eagerness.

Ethan raises his eyebrows at me, and I shoot him a secretive smile. I'm not sure why I didn't think of it before, but on the cab ride over, I made a couple of quick calls. Two out of the three celebrities I had time to contact were interested in backing Ethan's idea financially. Which, in hindsight, makes perfect sense since they believed in the project enough to endorse it in the video.

"What do you say, gentlemen?" I glance at my watch as if I have other, more important places to be—a tactic I'd seen my dad employ in countless client meetings.

Steel Suit murmurs something to the man seated on his left, just low enough that I can't make it out, then meets my eye. "We'll write up the contracts today. Is that soon enough?"

"Ethan?" I ask, making sure everyone knows that he's the one in charge.

He still looks a little dazed but manages a nod. "That sounds acceptable."

"Excellent. We'll have the contracts sent to you by messenger by the end of the day." Steel Suit stands, followed by his underlings, and they file out of the room, leaving Ethan and me alone.

In the wake of their departure, we face each other in silence, Ethan gazing at me with a mixture of bewilderment, awe, and utter exhilaration.

"That went pretty well, don't you think?" I say with a shy grin, suddenly feeling vulnerable now that the rush of the pitch is over.

"That's an understatement," he breathes, taking a tentative step toward me. "I can't believe you're here."

"I can't believe I almost missed it." For a moment, I forget we're standing in a rectangular fishbowl, our every action visible by the men and women on the other side of the solid glass wall. I bridge the gap between us, just short of flinging myself into his arms. I'm dying to touch him, to hold him close, but I relinquished that right when I fled. Instead, I open the web browser on Brynn's laptop and type in the address for the website we created together, the one I'd been using as an online journal. "There's something I'd like you to read."

When I turn the screen toward him, he blinks in surprise. "Your blog? But you wanted to keep that private."

"I did. But now, I'd like you to read my last entry."

He leans forward, then hesitates. "You're sure?"

"Don't make me read it out loud," I threaten in a teasing tone, although I'm not sure I could, even if I tried. Not without dissolving into a blubbering mess. Unlike Veronica, I'm *not* a pretty crier.

He presses his palm on the table, stooping to read the small box of text.

I hold my breath, recalling every nuance of what I wrote, down to each individual comma, as his eyes scan back and forth across the screen.

Today, I told my dad that New York is my home, where I belong. But I didn't tell him why. It's not because it has this vibrant, surging energy that ignites a sense of optimism, as if anything is possible. It's not because there are pockets of wonder and magic scattered all throughout the city, evoking awe and amazement when you least expect it. And it's not because it's a living, breathing entity that's constantly teaching me something new, shaping me into a better version of myself.

I love all those things about this extraordinary city, but it's not what makes it home. What makes it home is Ethan. He enriches my life simply by being in it. His steadfast presence is like an anchor, but instead of cementing me in place, he keeps me rooted to what really matters, so I can grow and reach and climb without losing myself along the way.

I belong in New York because I belong with Ethan. And I

only regret that it took me this long—a lifetime, really—to realize it.

When Ethan finishes reading, he looks up, searching my face. His hazel eyes are like a lucent window into his soul, and a pleasant shiver ripples through me when I glimpse the tender intensity reflected back at me.

"I'm so sorry I left without saying goodbye," I say softly, holding his gaze even though my knees are trembling. "And I'm so sorry I left without saying..." I pause, my breath shallow and raspy as I whisper, "I love you, too."

Without a word—and without a single thought of someone watching through the window—Ethan cups my face with his hand, kissing away every lingering doubt until all that remains is an overwhelming desire to spend each waking second exactly like this one.

"Let's go home," he murmurs against my lips, and I might actually melt onto the floor if not for his arm looped around my waist.

Realistically, I know the three of us can't live together forever. Ethan rooming with Brynn was always meant to be temporary, and I have a feeling, considering his burgeoning success, he'll be finding his own place soon, embarking on a new chapter with new possibilities.

New. Another word, like *home*, that used to evoke mixed feelings, at once exciting and terrifying. But now

I've come to view it as the former, embracing change with hopeful expectation.

After all, in a glittering, glorious city like New York, surrounded by the people you love, the future can't be anything but bright.

EPILOGUE

Sometimes in life, we're gifted a moment that seems to stand still, like a photograph forever framed in our minds. This is one of those moments. My family—Mom, Dad, Matt, and Veronica—are seated around the fire, sipping from monogrammed mugs of hot chocolate, while Brynn and her parents converse in front of the large picture window. Their silhouettes are backlit by the city lights, hazy and ethereal, delicately diffused by the softly falling snow. Brynn's father, Dennis, stoops to untangle Whiskers from the long scarf I'd knit her for Christmas, the one Wilson now uses to tow her around our apartment.

Our apartment.... Although Brynn and I have only been official roommates for eight months, it's hard to remember a time when we didn't live together, when I didn't call this place home.

Ethan moved into his own apartment the second

MAD Market took off, as I knew it would. And once the festive frenzy of holiday shopping began, its popularity soared beyond even our most auspicious expectations.

It's hard to describe how it feels to see his dreams finally come to fruition—to witness the result of all his hard work, striving for such a worthy cause—but I can say this: it's an intoxicating combination of unabashed pride and unrelenting joy and delight. The exhilaration has even trickled into my own endeavors since the success of MAD Market's ad campaign helped to launch the East Coast branch of Carmichael Creatives. In fact, in the new year, we'll be moving into a bigger office and hiring additional staff. So far, it's only been me and my part-time assistant, Jenny, and I mostly work from home unless I'm meeting with a client.

"Wow. It smells incredible in here."

I turn toward the smooth, scintillating sound of Ethan's voice. My heart still flutters at the sight of him. He unhooks Wilson's leash, hanging it on the hook by the door before shrugging out of his heavy wool coat. Even in his aunt Myrtle's latest monstrosity—a chunky cable-knit sweater with a deranged-looking elf embroidered on the front—he's the most attractive, utterly enticing man I've ever seen. Junior high me would be so jealous.

He dusts snowflakes out of his hair before striding into the kitchen to place a kiss on my cheek, wrapping his arms around my waist from behind. As we stand facing the stove, I lean against him, reveling in the strong, solid pressure of his body against mine. His woodsy scent mixes with the aroma of fresh basil and roasted garlic, and I breathe deeply, shivering with pleasure as he nuzzles my neck, pressing his warm lips against a particularly sensitive spot.

"Can you please save the public displays of affection until after dinner?" Matt groans, startling us both. "I'm starting to lose my appetite."

"Oh, leave them be," Veronica says, swatting his arm. "It's sweet."

I can't help smiling at her response, which is so different from our past interactions. Ever since she started dating Trent—a sitcom writer she met at her gym six months ago, who's since moved to New York to write for *Saturday Night Live*—she's become a shameless lover of love. Almost nauseatingly so, not that I'd tell her that. Directing her question to me, she asks, "Can we help with dinner?"

"That's code for *hurry up, we're hungry*," Matt interjects in a teasing tone while itching his nose, a mild symptom of his dog allergy that wasn't alleviated by the Benadryl. Of course, it's partially his own fault. Instead of keeping his distance, he became enamored by Wilson instantly, and has spent half the evening playing fetch and doling out head scratches.

"It's almost ready." I slip on a pair of oven mitts. "Can you grab serving spoons for the side dishes and set them on the table? Oh, and fill the water glasses."

"Sure thing." Veronica sweeps into the kitchen,

moving about the space with all the ease and familiarity befitting her frequent visits. I have a feeling if things continue to move quickly with Trent, it's only a matter of time before she becomes a permanent fixture around here. She's even hinted at the possibility of working together, which would technically make me her boss. A prospect that would've been laughable last Christmas. But now? I don't hate the idea of spending more time together.

While Veronica and Matt place the scalloped potatoes, green salad, biscuits, and roasted asparagus on the table, I slide the main course out of the oven.

Ethan's mouth tips into a smile, the slightly slanted smile that makes my limbs wobbly. "While I'm still partial to the first one you made me, I rather like this new Christmas tradition of ours."

"Me, too." I beam at the festive frittata, my heart swelling with happiness and a twinge of pride. Although the spinach I'd carefully arranged had shriveled in the heat, the leaves maintained their tree-like shape, and the scattered slices of red, yellow, and green bell pepper perfectly resemble a colorful array of ornaments. I may not be competing on any cooking shows anytime soon, but I've made a lot of progress. And not only in the kitchen.

The aroma draws the rest of our family over to our makeshift dining room, and while Brynn serves Whiskers and Wilson their special baked salmon, I set the hot skillet on a trivet at the head of the table.

Over dinner, Matt regales us with humorous anecdotes culled from his new role as marketing director while Dad updates us on his semiretirement, which really means he conducts more business meetings on the golf course. Brynn's mom, Colleen, tells us about her new personalized sock-gnome business, which is exactly what it sounds like—gnomes made out of socks, custom-made to look like your loved ones. Apparently, they've become an internet sensation among young influencers. Who would've thought?

After dinner, we retire to the living room for dessert—more hot chocolate, pecan pie, and, of course, Mom's fruitcake. Ethan serves us a slice to share, and sacrificially chokes down most of it. Could the man be more wonderful?

While we cuddle on the couch, my gaze wanders to the row of gingerbread houses lining the console table along the back wall. Matt's re-creation of Hearst Castle, an ambitious feat even for him, Veronica's yurt, inspired by her recent yoga retreat, Brynn's Empire State Building, complete with candy cane spire, and Ethan's edible homage to the Brooklyn Bridge. All masterpieces in their own right. Then there's mine.

Since my humble cottage collapsed, I decided to change tack. Using two Oreo-flavored candy canes for their black and white stripes, plus cinnamon gummy bears squished and reshaped to mimic tiny red shoes—albeit slightly mangled shoes—I replicated Dorothy's house, post tornado, atop the Wicked Witch of the East.

In what will surely go down in history as a Christmas miracle, our parents collectively voted to crown my gingerbread house the winner thanks to its creativity and originality. But although I can finally claim the trophy—in all its cheap plastic, faux-gold glory—it doesn't hold the same level of significance that it once did. As cheesy as it sounds, I've already won in all the ways that matter.

I snuggle closer to Ethan, resting my head against his shoulder as my mother passes out the Christmas Commitments scrolls, including four blank ones so Ethan, Brynn, and their parents can join our quirky custom. *Lucky them.*

As I unfurl my scroll, my heart flutters. It's so surreal to see the last ten items marked off after so many years of sitting anxiously, listening to everyone else's accomplishments, knowing I'd failed. This year, for the first time ever, I can join in the celebration. I almost don't know what to do with myself.

"Can I share my Christmas Commitment?" Ethan asks, setting down his pen.

"We usually wait until next year," I tell him, although his enthusiasm is endearing.

"I think we can make an exception," Dad says, his eyes twinkling.

"Q, would you mind reading it for me?" Ethan hands me his scroll.

Is it my imagination, or is his jaw flexing ever so slightly?

"Sure," I say slowly, wondering why everyone is suddenly staring at me as if I'm about to announce the Powerball winners. Clearing my throat, I squint at his crisp, blocky handwriting. My mouth goes dry. Does it really say what I *think* it says?

My gaze flies to his face, my breath hitching as he drops to one knee.

There's something shiny and metallic poised between his fingers.

It's a ring. The most unique and entrancing engagement ring I've ever seen.

The matte yellow gold setting is elegant and subdued, while the raw, uncut diamond in the center speaks to my very soul.

I'm not sure how much time has passed, since it seems to have stopped altogether, but Ethan murmurs softly, "What does it say?"

"It—it says, Marry Quincy Carmichael." As I share his Christmas Commitment aloud, I don't think I've ever heard a combination of words so blissfully sweet in all my life.

I glance around the room, surprised to find everyone grinning, as if they'd known all along.

"What do you say, Q?" Ethan asks, drawing my gaze back to his. "Will you spend forever with me?"

Blinking back tears, I lift my pen and scribble something on my scroll, then pass it to Ethan.

He takes one glance and slips the ring on my finger, pulling me into his arms for a kiss so ardent and all-consuming, I don't even hear our family's cheers and applause.

In the commotion, the scroll flutters to the floor, my Christmas Commitment facing up for all the world to see.

And this time, I've chosen one I can't wait to complete.

WANT TO READ MORE BOOKS BY RACHAEL BLOOME? Visit her website at www.rachaelbloome.com and click subscribe to download free bonus content.

ACKNOWLEDGMENTS

First, I want to thank my readers. As I mentioned in my letter, I know this isn't the book you expected me to release next. And I know you've been patiently waiting for the next Poppy Creek and Blessings Bay books. I appreciate you sticking with me as I try something new and go where the "muse" takes me. This was exactly the mental break I needed before I sit down to write the final (for now) installment of Poppy Creek. So again, thank you for indulging my writerly whims. I had so much fun writing Quincy's story, and I hope you enjoyed it, too.

To Mariah Sinclair—Thank you for the stunning premade cover that sparked the idea for this story. I fell in love the second I saw it, and I'm so honored to publish your beautiful design.

To Krista Dapkey—Thank you for your generous willingness to work with my chaotic life and utter lack of anything closely resembling a "schedule." You're the best.

To Beth Attwood—Thank you for squeezing me in at the last minute, adding the extra polish that makes the prose shine, and catching those pesky continuity errors that slip through the cracks.

To Dave Cenker—You've been a steady critique partner since the beginning, and I'm seriously starting to question if I can publish a book without you. Your insights mean the world to me.

To my family—Your continued support of my writing dream is the backbone of my business. I'm so deeply grateful that I can share it with you, from the constant bookish chats to towing you across the country to reader retreats and book signings. Unlike Quincy, I have the most loving and selfless family in the world. Although, for some of us, good-natured teasing is definitely our love language.

ABOUT THE AUTHOR

Rachael Bloome is a *hopeful* romantic. She loves every moment leading up to the first kiss, as well as each second after saying, "I do." Torn between her small-town roots and her passion for traveling the world, she weaves both into her stories—and her life!

Joyfully living in her very own love story, she enjoys spending time with her husband, adorable daughter, and two rescue dogs, Finley and Monkey. When she's not writing, helping to run the family coffee roasting business, or getting together with friends, she's busy planning their next big adventure!

BOOK CLUB QUESTIONS

1. What did you think of the Carmichael's Christmas Commitments tradition? Have you ever made a similar list, be it resolutions or a bucket list? If so, what are some of the items you included?

2. How is your family dynamic similar or dissimilar to the Carmichaels? Can you relate to any of their quirks/quarrels?

3. Have you ever struggled with perfectionism? Or the desire to be "perfect"?

4. Do you enjoy trying new things? Or do you find them intimidating? Is there anything on Quincy's list that you'd like to try?

5. What are your thoughts around the subject of quitting? When is it okay to quit something and when should you stick with it?

6. New York City plays a big role in the story. Have you ever visited? If so, what were your favorite sights/experiences? If not, would you like to visit?

7. How did you feel about Quincy and Ethan's relationship? Do you think they make a good couple? Why or why not?

9. Quincy struggled with self-confidence and realizing she had her own unique gifts and talents to offer the world. What would you say is one of your special gifts?

10. What do you think is the main theme of the story?

As always, I'd love to hear your thoughts. You can email your responses (or ask your own questions) at hello@rachaelbloome.com or post them in my private Facebook group, Rachael Bloome's Secret Garden Club.

Made in the USA
Monee, IL
11 November 2024

69844842R00144